Gone Was The Charming, Funny And Highly Sensual Man She'd Just Danced With, And In His Place Stood A Man Of Stone.

"What's wrong?" she whispered to him.

Bobby acted as though he hadn't heard her. He stared at her brother Sakir, his gaze hooded like a hawk.

"Is it possible for us to behave like gentlemen tonight, Callahan?" Sakir asked, his tone cool as he stuck out a hand in Bobby's direction.

Eyes narrowed, Bobby glowered.

"It'll be a cold day in hell before I shake the hand of the man who stole my father's land and helped put him in the ground."

Dear Reader,

Welcome to another fabulous month of novels from Silhouette Desire. Our DYNASTIES: THE ASHTONS continuity continues with Kristi Gold's *Mistaken for a Mistress*. Ford Ashton sets out to find the truth about who really murdered his grandfather and believes the answers may lie with the man's mistress—but who is Kerry Roarke *really*? *USA TODAY* bestselling author Jennifer Greene is back with a stellar novel, *Hot to the Touch*. You'll love this wounded veteran hero and the feisty female whose special touch heals him.

TEXAS CATTLEMAN'S CLUB: THE SECRET DIARY presents its second installment with *Less-than-Innocent Invitation* by Shirley Rogers. It seems this millionaire rancher has to keep tabs on his ex-girlfriend by putting her up at his Texas spread. Oh, poor girl…trapped with a sexy—wealthy—cowboy! There's a brand-new KING OF HEARTS book by Katherine Garbera as the mysterious El Rey's matchmaking attempts continue in *Rock Me All Night*. Linda Conrad begins a compelling new miniseries called THE GYPSY INHERITANCE, the first of which is *Seduction by the Book*. Look for the remaining two novels to follow in September and October. And finally, Laura Wright winds up her royal series with *Her Royal Bed*. There's lots of revenge, royalty and romance to be enjoyed.

Thanks for choosing Silhouette Desire. In the coming months be sure to look for titles by authors Peggy Moreland, Annette Broadrick and the incomparable Diana Palmer.

Happy reading!

Melissa Jeglinski

Melissa Jeglinski
Senior Editor
Silhouette Desire

Please address questions and book requests to:
Silhouette Reader Service
U.S.: 3010 Walden Ave., P.O. Box 1325, Buffalo, NY 14269
Canadian: P.O. Box 609, Fort Erie, Ont. L2A 5X3

HER ROYAL BED

LAURA WRIGHT

Silhouette®

Desire

Published by Silhouette Books

America's Publisher of Contemporary Romance

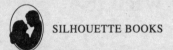 **SILHOUETTE BOOKS**

ISBN 0-373-76674-2

HER ROYAL BED

Copyright © 2005 by Laura Wright

Printed in U.S.A.

Books by Laura Wright

Silhouette Desire

Cinderella & the Playboy #1451
Hearts Are Wild #1469
Baby and the Beast #1482
Charming the Prince #1492
Sleeping with Beauty #1510
Ruling Passions #1536
Locked Up with a Lawman #1553
Redwolf's Woman #1582
A Bed of Sand #1607
The Sultan's Bed #1661
Her Royal Bed #1674

LAURA WRIGHT

has spent most of her life immersed in the world of acting, singing and competitive ballroom dancing. But when she started writing romance, she knew she'd found the true desire of her heart! Although born and raised in Minneapolis, Laura has also lived in New York City, Milwaukee and Columbus, Ohio. Currently she is happy to have set down her bags and made Los Angeles her home. And a blissful home it is—one that she shares with her theatrical production manager husband, Daniel, and three spoiled dogs. During those few hours of downtime from her beloved writing, Laura enjoys going to art galleries and movies, cooking for her hubby, walking in the woods, lazing around lakes, puttering in the kitchen and frolicking with her animals. Laura would love to hear from you. You can write to her at P.O. Box 5811, Sherman Oaks, CA 91413 or e-mail her at laurawright@laurawright.com.

One

Jane Hefner affixed an easy smile to her face as she walked into the entryway of Rolley Estate, her heels clicking against the white marble. One month ago, the Turnbolts' grand Texas compound would have made her normally confident manner wilt slightly. But that was one month ago, when she'd been a regular girl, living in a modest duplex on a quiet street of an even quieter beach town in California, working as a chef in a quaint little restaurant for a meager salary—a salary she'd hoped would someday earn her enough to open her own sand-side eatery.

One month ago, when she'd been just Jane Hefner—not Jane Hefner Al-Nayhal, the long-lost princess of a small but wealthy country named Emand.

With only four weeks worth of instructed grace and

poise to her credit, Jane shouldered her way through the thick crowd now milling about the Turnbolts' mahogany-paneled living room snatching up a variety of hors d'oeuvres and what her mother always referred to as "stiff drinks."

Rolley Estate was a magnificent place, a massive hunting-lodge-style home that sat atop a twelve-hundred-foot tall mesa overlooking four thousand acres of prime wildlife habitat. Just thirty minutes outside of Paradise, Texas, Rolley felt a world away from the big city with its quiet serenity, native game and rugged beauty. Jane had learned from her brother that the owners, Mary Beth and Hal Turnbolt, had purchased the property five years previously and had quickly transformed the once-unhurried surroundings into a modern showplace complete with three guesthouses, a lake and gazebo, a show barn, an indoor arena and a helipad.

Finding a relatively quiet spot near the brick fireplace, Jane sat, the gentle blaze behind her warming the skin of her back, which was laid bare due to the low sweep of her emerald-green silk dress. Lord, it felt wonderful to be alone. Even for just a few hours. She adored her new brothers and her sister-in-law, Rita, but in four weeks the only time she hadn't been engaged in conversation or some type of royal duty was in bed—and even then her dreams seemed to be just as active as her daily life.

"Shrimp?"

Jane glanced up and smiled at the friendly-looking waiter, remembering why she was attending the Turnbolts' party—to check out the high-society Tex-Mex party food, wait staff and chefs in Dallas. She had a staff to hire and a menu of her own to create. Baby Daya Al-Nayhal's Welcome to the World party was just three weeks away, and Jane was determined to make Sakir's and Rita's jaws drop when they saw the spread.

Reaching for a large grilled shrimp, Jane eyed a small bowl of untouched sauce beside the fan of prawns. "What's this?"

"Oh." The young man bit his lip, his gaze flickering from Jane to the sauce, then back again. "That's cilantro. A cream sauce, I think."

He thinks?

Jane grimaced. If this guy worked in her kitchen she'd be reading him the riot act right now. But she didn't have a kitchen of her own anymore.

"Would you like to try it?" The question held a touch of worry, as if the man hadn't tried the sauce himself and wasn't altogether sure about the freshness of the main ingredients.

"Thank you," Jane said, sliding a half dozen shrimp onto her plate.

The sauce was divine, spicy and creamy and a definite asset to the shrimp. As she watched her uninformed waiter walk away, then sidle up to an older couple with his silver tray, Jane shook her head. She felt for the chef whose delicious concoction was going unnoticed as the waiter not only forgot to offer it, but also looked uneasy about ingredients he couldn't even name.

Finishing off one large prawn, Jane wondered if her search for catering staff might prove more difficult than she had once thought. If the past week was any indication, then she ought to start worrying. Three parties in seven days and she'd found only one server who had made an impression on her. There was no doubt about it. She had to focus every ounce of her time and energy on the search, with no other interests to distract her. The problem was, she was finding herself distracted a lot lately. Granted, she was happy to offer herself as caterer to her new family for this one event, but that fulfilling surge of pride and purpose wasn't there, as it had been when she was a chef.

Jane's thoughts faltered as around her the noise in the room dropped to a dull roar. She glanced up and saw a woman in her late sixties with dark eyes and a very long, beakish nose standing at a makeshift podium, two priceless abstract oil paintings hanging impertinently on either side of her. It was their hostess, Mary Beth Turnbolt. She stared at the crowd as though she would dearly love to press some invisible mute button and get everyone to quit talking. But she did just as well by lifting her hands in the air and pursing her thin lips.

"Ladies and gentlemen," she began to say in a husky, though surprisingly friendly voice. "I would like to thank you for coming tonight. It's wonderful to see so many friends who support this cause. As most of you know, our housekeeper Beatrice's son, Jesse, is afflicted with Down's Syndrome, and Hal and I are just as passionate as his parents about funding research and treatments."

Jane saw Mary Beth turn and smile at a round, apple-cheeked blond woman sitting on the couch. A man Jane could only assume was Beatrice's husband sat beside her, his hand clamped tightly over hers.

Jane felt a pull of emotion as she fully realized the weight of the evening's benefit.

"We have a special guest tonight," Mary Beth continued, drawing Jane's gaze back to the podium. "He rarely comes to these events, though we all try to persuade him."

A trickle of soft feminine laughter followed this comment, and Jane's brows drew together in confusion.

Mary Beth beamed, her smile large and toothy. "Please help me welcome one of my dear friends, and the man who trained all nine of our horses, Bobby Callahan."

Jane followed the gazes of the party guests as all eyes flew to the doorway. It didn't take long to see what all the tittering and whispering was about. Promptly forgetting about the three remaining shrimp drowning in delectable sauce on her plate, Jane stared at the man walking through the crowd and up to the podium. He was in his early thirties, at least six-foot-three, brawny and barrel-chested, and wearing a black tuxedo that could barely contain him.

Jane's heart began to thump, and the easy blaze behind her suddenly felt like an all-consuming forest fire.

Unlike most of the dressed-up testosterone in the room, this was no society gentleman who stood before her. His cowboy swagger and rugged, untamed features under a short crop of dark-brown hair, clearly stated that this man worked outside, pushed his body to the limit and didn't give a damn about designer labels or fancy shrimp.

Jane remembered to swallow as Bobby Callahan faced the crowd with a self-assured, denim-blue stare.

He was far from classically handsome, but the air he gave off—that gust of leather and sunshine and pure-blooded male—easily made him the sexiest man in the room.

Jane watched as he adjusted the microphone to accommodate his height, then placed his large hands on either side of the podium. "First off, I want to thank Mary Beth and Hal for giving this party to help Down's Syndrome and KC Ranch. And I want to thank them for inviting me here tonight and allowing me to speak to y'all. Especially knowing how long-winded I can get." He paused, gave a decidedly roguish smile.

Jane stood and on bizarrely unsteady legs, moved into the crowd, closer to the podium.

"My daddy used to say," Bobby began to say, his sexy Texan drawl as big as the rest of him. "'If it don't seem like it's worth the effort, it probably ain't.' Those words have stuck with me, made me look real close, find out what's important in this life." He inhaled deeply, then continued talking in a powerful voice, "Most of you know that my sister, Kimmy, died one month ago today. She was the inspiration for KC ranch, and the most important thing in my life, and I miss her every damn minute. But her memory gives me a reason, a kick in the backside actually, to get up in the morning. Sure, she had Down's, but she never let that stop her. She was a tough one, bossed me around somethin' awful. But she was my best friend, and my inspiration." His voice fell from booming to restrained, and his grin vanished. He looked around, nodded at a few people before resuming. "Some of you know about KC Ranch—the morning grooming programs we offer for the little kids, the after-school assisted-riding programs and overnight summer camps for developmentally challenged, hearing-impaired, learning-disabled, physically challenged and visually impaired kids. Some of you have been real generous over the years, and some of you may decide to get real generous tonight."

There was a collective chuckle sprinkled throughout the room, though the sound was respectfully muffled. Bobby Callahan was absolutely riveting, grabbing the men's attention with his humor and easy speech, and the women's with his honorable words, and the loyalty and love he had for his sister.

"I believe, and I know my dad would've felt the same, that KC Ranch is worth every effort." His jaw tightened as he nodded. "Hope y'all do, too. Have a good night now."

The room erupted into applause, and Jane noticed that some of the women were dabbing at their eyes, trying to stop their fifty-dollar mascara from running. But she didn't keep her gaze on the crowd for long. Standing on her tiptoes, she strained to find Bobby Callahan, to see where he was, and if he was with anyone.

She couldn't get over his speech, those words, they'd torn into the open wound of her soul, the one that had never healed since her mother had told her so many years ago that she was going blind. It was odd. Many people had tried to talk with Jane about her mother, about her feelings and fears over the years. But Jane always had stuffed her emotions. She'd never had the time or the fortitude to go there in her mind and heart. But tonight, for some strange reason, Bobby Callahan had dug up all of those long-buried feelings.

Her pulse jumping in her blood, Jane spotted him shaking hands with a few people at the bar before grabbing two beers and heading out of the room.

Jane waited to see if anyone would follow him, and when no one did, she made her move.

"Spare rib in a port-wine glaze?" A girl in her early twenties with a killer tan and wide green eyes, a shade lighter than Jane's, held out a silver tray. "Goes wonderfully with the dry merlot we're serving tonight."

Jane shook her head, distracted. "No, thank-you." The server was perfect—in appearance, attitude and professionalism—and if Jane was on top of things, she would have found out the girl's name and phone number for the Welcome to the World party. But the focus she'd sworn to uphold just moments ago had evaporated when Bobby Callahan had taken the stage.

Normally she wasn't this interested. Normally she looked at men as a consideration for the future, possible husband material, a father to the three children she wanted to have someday. Normally she didn't leave a party to hunt down a tall, tanned and highly altruistic cowboy. But tonight she was pulled from the room by some unknown force she was too mortified, and frankly too scared, to name.

Ten minutes of searching and careful inquiries later, she found him. One floor up, and down a long hallway, a large flagstone terrace jutted out over the preserve. A soft, though oddly cool breeze for early fall, rustled in the trees beyond, and made Jane hug her arms.

The man whose words had been so heartfelt and animated downstairs was now standing against the railing, reveling in the silence of the landscape, drinking a beer, his back to her. Like some kind of deranged spy, Jane crept onto the deck and ducked behind a large potted plant. With no clue as to what her next move should be, she just watched him for a good five minutes as he downed both of his beers and stared into the black night.

Her right foot went tingly and her knees ached with the strain of her weight as she crouched there. She wondered what the hell she was thinking. Where had her good, practical and highly steady sense escaped to?

She glanced behind her. If someone saw her out here like this, she'd be the laughing stock of Paradise, Texas, and the surrounding counties, while embarrassing her brother and sister-in-law to no end.

What she needed to do was stand up, silently edge her way out of the plant and return to the party. Hey, if she really was desperate to meet Bobby Callahan there were about five more sensible ways of going about it.

"My daddy used to say," came a deep, masculine drawl, "'Never approach a bull from the front, a horse from the rear'." He turned around and eyed the potted plant as if he could see straight through it. "'Or a fool from any direction.' Which one you reckon I am?"

Jane went cold and her breath caught in her throat as a leaf pitilessly tickled her back.

"If you've got something to say, darlin', I suggest you come out from behind those weeds and say it."

Sweat broke out at the base of her skull where her dark brown hair was pinned neatly in a knot. It trickled down her neck into the bodice of her gown. What should she do now? Run for her life? Pretend she wasn't there? What if he stalked over to the plant, wrenched the leaves apart and caught her sitting there like an enormous ladybug?

Closing her eyes, taking a deep breath, she attempted to slow her thudding heart. But the yoga technique did nothing, and she forced herself to stand. Embarrassed to her very core, she parted the green foliage and stepped out of the massive plant. Shaking her head, she managed to say a lame, "I'm sorry."

Jane quickly saw that Bobby Callahan had a way of assessing a person with one easy sweep from toe to top. "Who are you?" he asked.

"Jane," she answered him, brushing a small clot of dirt from her dress.

He lifted one dark brow. "Just Jane?"

"Wouldn't that be easier?" she said dryly. "For us both?"

"Maybe, but I don't like being at a disadvantage when I'm talking to someone." Seeing her confused expression, he grinned. "You know my name? Front and back?"

"Yes."

"All right then." He crossed his powerful arms over his chest. "Out with it."

"Jane. Hefner."

A surly grunt came from Bobby's throat. "Hefner?"

She shook her head. "Don't look so hopeful. There's no relationship to the man who runs the naked bunny magazine."

He chuckled, the smooth, low sound reverberating off her skin. "You get that a lot, huh?"

"You have no idea." A thought of changing her name to Al-Nayhal had crossed Jane's mind a time or two in the past month, but Hefner had been who she was for too long now. It was her mother's name, after all.

"So, Jane Hefner, you spy on people a lot?"

"No," she stated, quite serious in both tone and expression. And yet, he looked doubtful.

"I don't think I believe that," he said.

"It's true. In fact, you're my first." The words were out of her mouth in a blink, but she still hoped she could somehow retrieve them because Bobby's brows drifted upward suggestively.

His grin widened. "Your first, huh? How was I?"

She let out a groan. "This situation is becoming more and more humiliating every second I stand here."

"Does that mean you won't be doing this kind of thing again?"

"Not a chance."

"An end to the spying?"

She nodded. "I think that would be best. Obviously I can't handle the outcome."

"And which outcome is that? The verbal sparring or the mild inquisition?"

"Mild?" she asked with a touch of humor in her tone.

"Oh, c'mon," said Bobby, his eyes glinting with a dangerous blue fire. "A man has the right—no, the obligation, to find why he's being tailed. Even when it's a beautiful woman who's doing the tailing."

He was unbearably attractive, rough and used and slightly broken in spirit. Jane stood there, brazenly staring at him, wondering what it would be like to touch him, to run her fingers over his face, that stubborn jaw, that slash of a scar on his upper lip. She wondered if he would be rough with a woman in bed or achingly slow and deliberate. She wondered if he allowed anyone to comfort him when he grieved for his sister.

Such strange, diverse thoughts worried her, made her heart thud in her chest, made her belly feel warm and liquid, as though she'd swallowed a cup of sweet honey.

"So, was there something you wanted?" he asked, cutting into her private reverie, a faint smile playing on his lips.

"No," she said quickly, then retreated, shook her head. "Well, that's not true." How did she put it? "I was…interested in you."

"Was?"

"Am," she said without thinking.

"Is that so?" Smiling lazily, he leaned back against the railing.

"What you said tonight," she began, walking gingerly toward him. "What you said…about your sister, and how you feel about her…it really moved me."

His expression changed in an instant. Where there had been an easy, roguish grin, a dark, thin line now etched his mouth. "So you're not really interested in me. You came to find me out of pity."

"No," she said at once, wondering how he could have

misunderstood her so, wondering what was pushing her even to continue with this conversation.

He took a swallow of his beer, then muttered tersely, "The sad dog with no tail, right?"

"That's not it at all."

"Darlin', I've seen it before, and I'm not looking for anyone's pity."

Above them, the wind played with the clouds, blowing the pale-gray poufs over the stars and moon, while casting Bobby Callahan's face in an eerily sensual shadow. But Jane could see his eyes clearly enough. Dark, and hot with emotion. A quick shiver traveled her spine. She'd seen that look before, seen eyes that masked great pain and regret. She'd seen that look in herself and in her mother, right before Tara Hefner had lost her sight.

She took another step toward him. "You have it all wrong, Mr. Callahan—"

"I doubt it," he interrupted.

"I wasn't offering you pity."

"What are you offering then, Jane Hefner?"

The question startled her. So did his expression. Unmasked passion—though from anger or sexual curiosity, she wasn't sure.

She stood on legs filled with water and listened to her heart pound in her chest. What *did* she want from this man? To talk? To exchange painful histories and hopes for the future? That was an incredibly brazen thing to expect from a stranger, now wasn't it?

A pang of need snaked through her, through her belly, up to her breasts. It was a completely insane moment for her as she realized she wanted him to touch her, hold her against him.

She looked him straight in the eye and said in apologetic tones, "I feel like an idiot here. This kind of thing is all new to me. Like I said, I don't usually follow men out of parties, spy on them and offer to—"

"Again the offer," he broke in, his gaze riveted on her, his eyes an almost stormy shade of blue. "What is it you're offering, darlin'?"

A picture of his body against hers flashed into her brain, but she rejected it. For the moment. "I just thought you might want to talk."

He stared at her blankly. The deep-cut shadows beneath his eyes hinted at nights not spent in sleep. Was it grief that kept him awake or the soft body of a woman?

"I know what it feels like to lose someone," she said, in a quiet voice. She hadn't lost her mother physically, but in her own way she had. They hadn't been able to do the same things, share the same things. "I know the pressures of a family member who has a disability."

He said nothing at first, just looked at her…or straight through her, she couldn't tell which. Then he shook his head and muttered a terse, "Not into talking, Miss Hefner. Thanks, but no thanks."

"Mr. Callahan—"

"I'm not looking for a soulmate, and I sure as hell ain't looking for pity."

"You keep misunderstanding—"

He pushed away from the wall and covered the few feet between them. "Have a beer on you?"

"No."

"How 'bout a whiskey?"

She shook her head, tried mentally to slow her pulse as his closeness, his scent, had her heart in her throat. "No."

He shrugged, then suddenly reached out, took hold of her arm and hauled her against him. "Well, this'll do, I suppose."

Jane never had a chance to think, much less react as Bobby Callahan dipped his head and covered her mouth with his. As his lips crushed against hers, she felt her belly tighten, felt her knees cease to hold her weight. There was no slow sweetness about his kiss. He was all passion and fireworks, hungry as a wolf and frighteningly demanding.

For the first time in a month, Jane felt her mind go. His passion, anger, fear, whatever it was that had called her to him tonight, fused into her skin, branding her.

He moved impossibly closer. He was incredibly tall, and although Jane stood five-foot-eight, she still had to roll up to her toes to gain full contact. When she did, Bobby growled, deepened his kiss, clearly spurred on by her interest. Gripping her waist and back, he tilted his head and eased his tongue into her mouth.

When he pulled back, left her mouth, his gaze was fierce, but vulnerable. "Unless you can give me more of that, darlin', we're done here."

Breathless, her body shocked with electricity and heat, Jane tried to find her sense of reason, but it was lost. Completely evaporated into a sky of need. She had been kissed with such desperation, passion and ferocity, it was as though Bobby Callahan wanted to consume her. It was as though she'd been offered a chance to morph into a hawk for one night and fly without any fear or reason. Her thighs trembled, for God's sake.

She'd never offered herself to a man. Not like this. Brazen and uncomplicated.

Swallowing every last bit of unease, Jane curled a hand around his neck and tugged his head lower. But before Bobby reached her mouth, he uttered, "You sure?"

"Yes," she said in breathless tones.

"Because this'll go way past a kiss."

"I'm counting on it."

His dark gaze flickered to the doorway behind her. "We can't do this here."

Truth be told, she didn't care where they ended up. On the deck, in a bathroom, against the tiles of a shower. She wanted this man, this stranger. A raw desperation filled her, rationalized her actions. It was complete and utter madness, but she wanted to fuse herself with the one person who had unknowingly touched her soul, the place she hadn't allowed anyone to touch in years.

"Come with me."

He practically carried her away from the deck and down the hall, his mouth ravaging hers, nipping at her lips, tasting her. Several times, he pushed her back against the wall and kissed her, his thigh pressing between hers, nudging at the pulsing center of her body. Time seemed to slow as they rolled and jostled their way to wherever Bobby was leading. Then Jane heard a muffled click as a door opened. The room was dim, just a faint cast of moonlight through an open window. She had no idea if they were in a bedroom or an office, and she didn't care. Bobby's mouth was on hers again.

She heard him kick the door closed with his foot. "It's not locked," she uttered, her skin itching to be touched by large, rough hands.

"I know." He eased her onto the bed, then shouldered out of his tuxedo jacket and white shirt. Jane stared, her lips parted. Bobby's face remained in shadow, but his chest, that tanned, thickly muscled chest, lay bare, greedy fingers of moonlight washing over him.

When he lowered his head and Jane found his gaze, she smiled. "This will be far better than a beer, I can promise you that."

"Better be," Bobby said with a lazy grin, though the muscles in his arms were as taut as pulled rope.

"You'll let me know…"

"I'll guide you every step of the way, darlin'." Bobby was over her in seconds, his mouth on hers. But he only allotted her a few deep kisses before his head dipped, finding her pulse at the base of her neck. He nibbled at the spot, drew his tongue up the band of muscle. Jane sucked air between her teeth and plunged her fingers into his hair. Down he moved to her collarbone, his teeth grazing over the sensitive skin.

A hungry growl escaped his throat as he tugged the top of her dress down. She wore no bra, and he quickly bent his head, took one stiff nipple into his mouth and suckled deeply. Jane gasped in pleasure and dug her nails into his skull.

Bobby tugged and suckled her steadily, making her toes point and her thighs tremble. Jane squirmed and pressed her hips up, against the mound of his erection.

Bobby eased down her dress and discarded it somewhere on the floor, then returned to her breast, laving slow circles around her aching nipple. His hand slipped down, over her ribs where her heart thudded violently, over her flat belly and under the slip of underwear at her hips. Pure instinct took her, and Jane opened her thighs in response. It had been so long—two and half years to be exact—since a man had touched her. She'd almost forgotten what it felt like.

Though she wasn't sure she'd really been touched before now. Bobby Callahan was an expert. He had skill and an erotic passion she'd never experienced. His emotions were raw and exposed as he ravished her body, acting as though he wanted to consume her.

His mouth was on her jaw, her neck, as his hand moved over the curls between her legs, his middle finger dipping into the wet seam beneath. Jane's skin prickled, and her womb pulsed in anticipation. She pumped her hips, urging him to use his hands, his mouth, anything. She wanted him on top of her, splaying her thighs as wide as they would go. She wanted him inside her.

But he had other plans.

Chuckling softly, he found the swollen peak hidden inside her slick folds, and flicked the pink cleft lightly between his thumb and middle finger.

"Oh…please…" Jane uttered, her hips and legs jerking wildly as she felt herself on the brink of orgasm.

"That's right," he whispered in her ear, quickly slipping off her underwear. "Let it come, darlin'. Let yourself come."

Her hips thrust up, over and over as he nipped her

earlobe and skillfully circled the pulsing, ultra-sensitive nub. Jane's breathing went ragged, and sensing her urgency, Bobby thrust two fingers inside her.

Jane's breath hitched, and she closed around him, her buttocks squeezing as electric currents ran through her, faster and stronger until she cried out, her hands digging into the flesh of his chest.

Her climax softened only a touch while Bobby ripped off his pants and sheathed himself. Without missing a beat, his mouth found hers as one powerful hand caught her wrists and lifted her arms over her head. She felt him hard and thick against her, pressing solidly against the opening to her body. With one long driving stroke, he was inside her. He was large, but her muscles clamped around him, took him fully.

No slow thrusts followed. No soft kisses or whisperings of what was coming next. Bobby was really worked up, ready to take his own release and Jane wanted to hear how he sounded when he came.

She wrapped her legs around his waist and thrust upward, meeting every stroke he gave her. He felt like heaven, so powerful, hitting a spot inside her womb so foreign she bit her lip. She tasted blood, but didn't care. Bobby was riding her hard and she was close to climaxing again. She lowered her legs, then slapped her thighs together under his body so she was holding him inside her as tightly as possible, while he bucked against the ridge of her sex.

It was too much for them both. Jane went first, her climax harder and richer the second time, and Bobby followed, pumping furiously into the tight glove of her body until he thrust hard upward and held, releasing a dark groan along with the wet heat of his orgasm.

Sweat dampened the sheets, held their bodies together as outside the moon once again escaped the cover of a cloud and brilliant yellow light beamed into the room, as if to remind them that their encounter was coming to a close.

But Bobby didn't seem to have the same interpretation of the moon's movement. He gathered Jane against him, held her tightly and brushed a kiss over her forehead.

Jane rested her cheek on his chest, listening to the beat of his heart. "We should probably get up, get dressed and go back down to the party," she whispered, the hair on his chest tickling her cheek.

"Probably," he uttered.

But that was all he would say as the minutes ticked by and his breathing slowed. He'd given in to sleep, and for a moment, she wholeheartedly wished she could do the same. To wake up with Bobby, maybe make love a second time before this whole mad fantasy of an evening came to a close. But then reality started to pinch at her. She'd wanted to be close to this man, feel his energy, his pain, his mouth, and she had. What she needed to do now was rise, brush off the tiny flecks of shame she felt for allowing such a tryst to happen and leave.

Her breathing shallow, she disentangled herself from Bobby's warm and heavenly grasp and sat up. It took her only moments to slip back into her panties and her dress, which had been in a rumpled pile on the floor. Then she looked back at Bobby Callahan. He looked so appealing in the washed light of the moon, his dark, powerful body wrapped in the sheets.

A flash of memory assaulted her, brought shivers to her skin—hands, strong and large, exploring, tantalizing.

She almost cast aside all her good sense and crawled back into bed with him. But instead she covered him gently with a blanket, grabbed her heels and slipped from the room.

Two

She was an untamed beast with a spirited attitude, but it was her elegance and beauty that had his muscles flexing and his pulse pounding in his blood.

The burnt-orange sun dipped into the horizon as Bobby came to a quick stop in the dirt. The charcoal-gray mare trotting beside him followed suit, snorting and smacking the ground with her hoof. Breaking two-year-olds could be a boring process; weeks of training on the ground before you even thought about riding. And even after you did get to ride, there was still not all that much excitement in store. Very little bucking, and a rare thing to take a tumble.

But this lady, Bobby mused, giving the mare at his right an appreciative look—she was spectacular. Her eyes darted with excitement, as if she wanted him to challenge her nature and instincts.

Bobby reached around, pushed his finger into the horse's shoulder, then ribs and hip, grinning when she quickly understood to calmly step away from the pressure. Not a day went by when he wasn't breaking or training a horse for someone. It was how he made his living, how he kept the ranch going and the kids coming. Sure, the private donations were large, but they were also few and far between.

Bobby pulled on each side of the mare's mouth, softening her jaw. This mare was for Charlie Docks, a sweet old man who had a place just north of Paradise, and to whom Bobby had turned for help and humbling support when his father had died all those years ago. He wouldn't be seeing a bundle of cash for breaking Charlie's mare, though. The man didn't have much, but he had offered Bobby a nice, reliable old nag for the kids in exchange.

"That Charlie's gal?"

Bobby glanced up, pushed his Stetson back. "Yep."

Standing at the corral gate, his foot propped up on a steel rung, was Abel Garret. KC Ranch's foreman was almost as big as Bobby, but a sight older with short, graying blond hair, pale-green eyes and a time-worn face. Abel had never told Bobby his exact age, but Bobby had guessed he was somewhere in his fifties. Thing was, he could stick on a grizzly attitude if he had a mind to, and sometimes it made him seem older. Folks thought he was a curmudgeon, but losing a wife to another man could do that to a person.

"Pretty thing," Abel remarked.

Saddle pad in hand, Bobby gently and rhythmically slapped the dusty pad against the horse's side. "Sure is. Smart as a whip, too."

Abel lifted a brow. "You're getting paid for this, right?"

"So to speak."

Abel chuckled, took off his Stetson and plowed a hand through his hair. "Couple chickens and a quilt?"

"C'mon, now. The man's got nothing but a good wife and ten head of Angus. He needs a respectable horse."

"Sure he does. But we don't got all that much more."

Bobby scrubbed a hand over his face, barbed with a day's growth of beard. He wasn't a rich man, but he was comfortable, had food on his table and a good business that did good work. "We've got thirty-two head," Bobby said to Abel, an easy grin playing about his mouth. "And you've been more than a good wife to me."

Abel frowned. "Shut yer face, will ya?"

Chuckling, Bobby said, "You know that you're talking to your boss?"

"Yeah, I know it."

Bobby moved down the mare's body, gently slapping the pad against her muscular legs. "Janice Young is coming by today."

"Who?"

"Woman I met at the Turnbolts' charity event last week." A shot of heat went through Bobby at the memory. But it had nothing to do with Janice Young. As far as Bobby was concerned, he'd noticed only one woman that night. A woman with smoky-green eyes, hair down her back and legs so long he'd have sworn she could've wrapped them around him twice—a woman who had taken over his mind and his body for the past seven nights. Hell, he'd barely dropped on his bed at night before the visions of her slammed into his brain, before sweat broke out on his forehead and the lower half of him went hard as steel.

"Right," Abel said, the late-afternoon sun still pounding him full force. "Forgot to ask you about that shindig. How'd it go?"

"Pretty dull." Bobby was closemouthed about women, even with Abel.

"So why's this gal coming by?"

"Her husband's law firm is donating ten grand to KC Ranch."

"Well, we can sure use it," Abel uttered, then paused, eyed Bobby with an amused expression. "She want anything in return?"

Bobby swatted away a nagging fly. "She's pushing seventy, Abel."

"Don't matter. Every time you come back from one of them things the phone is ringing off the hook. And I always end up talking to 'em, trying to make them love-sick fillies understand you ain't at home." He shook his head, rolled his lips under his teeth. "Won't be your damn secretary, Callahan. Didn't sign on for that."

"No one asked you to talk to them, Abel. Just tell them to call back."

Abel muttered something unintelligible that involved him ripping off his Stetson and swatting it against his worn jeans.

Bobby stared pointedly at the older man. "We're

lucky people are calling, and we're damn lucky to get the funds. It's for the kids, and don't you forget it."

Abel looked as if Bobby had sucker-punched him. "I'd never forget that and you know it!"

Bobby tossed the pad on the ground. "Yeah, I know."

Neither one of them said anything, just stood there, uncomfortable. It was strange. When Kimmy was alive, they'd been a family—the three of them together for dinner and holidays, working the ranch. She'd always made them laugh, made sure they didn't take themselves so seriously. Bobby and Abel had struggled somewhat since her death, trying to find their footing, trying not to be so serious.

The memory of Kimmy, of her beautiful wide face and huge grin, those sky-blue eyes and her bossy ways, slammed into Bobby, made him feel breathless with pain for the recent loss.

Clearing his throat, Abel, pushed away from the steel gate. "I could use a beer. How 'bout you?"

Bobby gave a clipped nod and muttered, "Sounds good."

Beside Bobby, the mare snorted, her eyes flashing with a readiness for freedom Bobby understood all too clearly. She'd done well today. He gave her thigh a light smack and hollered. She took off toward Abel, who quickly opened the gate and allowed her to run past him, out into the pasture.

The men walked side by side toward the main house, their strides equally long and purposeful.

"Got another one 'round the corner, don't you?" Abel asked.

"What's that?" Bobby said.

"Another one of them charity things."

"Friday night." Bobby was dirty and dusty as hell. Not fit to look at, kind of like most days, but he wanted to see that woman again, right here, right now. He wondered if she'd be at that charity event. He wanted to see if she was real, if those emerald-green eyes of hers would once again streak with gray when he kissed her. He wanted to taste her again, do things he'd fantasized about doing ever since he'd woken up in an empty bed.

He sniffed and rolled his eyes as they went into the house and headed for the kitchen. He was acting like a real jackass with all this frilly thinking. He liked women, liked taking them to bed, and that night at the Turnbolts' shouldn't have been any different.

Except that it was.

He grabbed two cold beers from the fridge. On most occasions, one night of good, mutually pleasurable sex was enough for him. But Jane Hefner had wreaked havoc inside Bobby, and he wanted to see her again. Not only because he wanted to touch her, but because he wanted to know why the hell she'd left him. The question consumed him.

"Is it a tea party or fancy-dress ball?" Abel said, taking a chug of his beer.

Bobby's mouth tugged with humor as he leaned back against the counter. "Barbecue, actually."

Abel snorted. "Pulled pork and Oscar de la Whatshisname."

"I'm going to plug KC Ranch. That's all."

"'Course."

Bobby tipped his beer in Abel's direction and grinned. "You want to go?"

"I'll work for you, Bobby," Abel said, real slow and deliberate, "I'll even answer the phone for you on occasion—but I sure as hell won't date you."

"I have never seen you so nervous. What is wrong, my sister?"

The man before Jane was tall, dark, wealthy, charming and decadently handsome—he also had her eyes.

Sakir Al-Nayhal offered Jane his hand as she stepped out of the limousine. "I'm fine, Sakir, just keyed up."

"Keyed up?" Under his brand-new brown Stetson, his thick black brows drew together. "What is this, *keyed up?*"

Sakir's wife, Rita, laughed and slipped her arm through his. "She's excited, sweetheart."

"Why are you excited?" Sakir asked as they walked the short pathway to the Gregers' massive ranch house.

Jane mentally rolled her eyes. If her brother only knew what was making her pulse pound furiously and her breath hitch. But of course he didn't. With all of his focus going to his new daughter, his wife and his work, he'd barely acknowledged that his sister had gone to a charity function last week.

Jane, on the other hand, hadn't been able to stop thinking about the affair at the Turnbolts', and about Bobby Callahan. Those raw blue eyes haunted her dreams, as did that scar on his lip that she'd traced with her tongue, and the hot-blooded, hungry way he'd made love to her. If that was not enough, her thoughts would stray from his physical attributes to the more emotional queries, such as, had she done the right thing leaving without a word? And was that why he hadn't tried to find her, to ask her out again? Maybe he wasn't all that thrilled with her or the time they'd shared.

Her heart dropped into the brown distressed-leather boots she'd bought just that morning, along with a pair of jeans and a faded denim jacket. She wasn't all that experienced in the ways of lovemaking, but she knew this much—she'd been dangerously passionate with him that night.

It was a risky thing to let your imagination run wild, she decided as they stepped inside the Gregers' home and settled into the jovial crowd of exceedingly wealthy cowboys and cowgirls.

The interior of the ranch house looked like something out of *Home and Garden,* the Texas edition. This was no easy homestead as she'd imagined Bobby Callahan's KC Ranch to be, but an elegantly rustic home with beamed ceilings, gleaming hardwood floors covered in colorful rugs, a massive brick fireplace and a wall of glass that was now retracted to allow partygoers to use the sprawling backyard.

As Sakir led them outside where the real party seemed to be taking place, Jane's gaze darted here and there, looking for the tallest, largest and sexiest *real* cowboy in the crowd. He'd be here, wouldn't he? Texas society went to everything, didn't they? And he was a pretty sought-after member of the Dallas crowd, though selective about which parties he attended. She only knew this because of what Mary Beth Turnbolt had said in her speech that night, and the few articles she'd read about Bobby Callahan and his ranch on the Internet.

Excitement and nerves were forming mini tornados in her stomach as a concerned female voice uttered, "Jane?"

Jane forced her gaze back to her family. Rita was watching her, curiosity lighting her eyes. And Sakir seemed to be assessing her. Jane gave them both a bright smile. "You two enjoy yourselves. I'm going to work now, see if I can scrounge up some barbecue to taste, and a staff to interrogate."

"We don't want you working the whole party, Jane," Rita said, smoothing the skirt of her denim dress. "Do we, Sakir?"

"Jane must do as she thinks best, but it is fact that Al-Nayhals are most content when they are working."

Rita lifted an amused eyebrow. "Most content working, huh?"

A slow grin worked its way to Sakir's full mouth. "Work is contentment," he acknowledged, nodding, "while pleasure, amusement and overwhelming happiness are what I get from you, dearest."

On a laugh, Rita said, "That's better."

For a moment, Jane watched the pair. Just as it was with her eldest brother Zayad and Jane's best friend, Mariah, Sakir and Rita made love look so wonderful, so safe. She envied them all, wondered if such a blissful state would ever befall her.

"I'll see you both later, okay?"

Sakir nodded, and Rita smiled, said, "We'll meet you by the dance floor for dinner in, say, an hour?"

Jane nodded. "Sounds good."

As they walked away, Jane grinned at her brother in his jeans and boots, so completely bizarre-looking on a man who wore suits, expensive sportswear or a formal kaftan 24/7.

But they were both a long way from Emand and its edicts, weren't they? she thought, walking around the backyard, through the gardens and over to a circle of barbecues, where a crowd had gathered, inhaling the mouthwatering scents of hickory, beef and pork. Yes, she was away from her father's homeland and her mother's place in California. She was here in Texas, try-ing to decide where her life was going, where she be-longed and if she was ever going to realize her dream of opening her own restaurant.

She looked around. She didn't see any sign of Bobby Callahan, and with a flood of disappointment, she won-dered if he might not be coming. She'd dressed with such care, too, wearing a pretty green silk blouse, and she'd even spent a good twenty minutes on her hair and makeup.

Forcing back the melancholy snaking through her, she decided to concentrate on the real reason she was at the Gregers' party—to taste and talk, and potentially to employ.

By eight o'clock, she'd hired two waiters and an as-sistant chef for Sakir and Rita's party. She'd also tasted some of the best barbecue in her life. She was very pleased with herself, and quite preoccupied as she made her way to the dance floor to meet her brother and sis-ter-in-law—so preoccupied in fact that she hardly no-ticed when someone put a hand on her shoulder.

But the voice, that deep, sensual timbre, sent her reeling back to a night of careless, heedless passion—one of the best nights of her life.

"You look beautiful tonight, darlin'."

Jane turned around, her breath hitching. He stood before her, the man she'd given up hope she'd see tonight, an easy smile on his face. She looked him over greedily. He wore a pair of worn dress boots with faded jeans that hugged his powerful thighs and, under a caramel suede jacket, a blue shirt made his chest look a mile wide, while the color made his eyes pop.

He pinched the tip of his stone-colored Stetson and gave her a nod.

She felt like a teenager, all nervousness and thrill. "Hello."

"Hello?" he repeated, his grin, sexy. "That's all I get?"

Playing along, she cocked her head to the side. "What more do you want?"

He shrugged. "How about a few answers to a few questions?"

"I'll do my best."

"Want to tell me why you up and left me in the middle of the night?"

The question took the breath from her, and she forced a smile. "Jumping right into it, are we?"

"Why not?"

"All right." She shook her head. "I thought it might be best if I wasn't caught in nothing more than a sheet in the house of—"

"You were in more than a sheet, darlin'," he interrupted with a grin. "Had my arms around you, didn't I?"

She laughed. "Is my face red? Because it sure feels like it is."

"Your face is fine. Beautiful actually."

Warmth curled in her belly, and around them the room spun slowly, the noise of the crowd dulled. "As I was saying, I thought it might be best if I wasn't caught in nothing more than a sheet...et cetera." She grinned as he laughed again. "We were in a stranger's bedroom, after all."

"Hardly a stranger," Bobby corrected. "Hal and Mary Beth have been friends of mine for a long time."

"*Your* friends, not mine," she pointed out.

"They're very nice people. They'd have embraced you."

"Something that would've been good to know nine days ago."

"Ten," he corrected.

Jane stared at him, into those soulful blue eyes of his, and felt her breasts tighten, felt the muscles between her thighs tingle. So, he had thought about her, had counted the days, had wanted to see her again.

She cleared her throat. "So the Turnbolts didn't ask why you'd fallen asleep in one of their guest rooms? Naked?"

"They thought I'd just tied one on."

"Ah."

"They were real hospitable. Eggs, bacon and fresh-squeezed orange juice in the morning."

"Sounds good," said Jane, as behind her, the band leader announced a two-step.

"Not as good as a different morning activity might've been." He laughed at her stunned expression. "Before I scare you away with all my innuendo and good-old-boy frankness, have a dance with me."

"I don't know this kind of dancing."

He took her hand in his and led her out on the floor. "Trust me, Jane Hefner."

She smiled at him and slipped her hand in his. "But I hardly know you, Bobby Callahan."

He grinned. "Boy, we're gonna have to remedy that, don't you think?"

"Yes, I think so." She'd never flirted so outrageously in her life—but of course, as far as Bobby Callahan went, she seemed to be racking up a laundry list of firsts.

He moved with masculine grace, slow, sexy, making sure she was taken care of as they circled the floor. At one point the music came to a twangy crescendo and he led her into a slow turn, then pulled her back into his arms. "So you know why I come to these things—to help out my ranch—but why are you here? You're not a society lady, are you?"

"No," she said, slightly breathless as she felt his chest brush against the tips of her breasts. "I'm a chef."

"Oh, a woman who can cook," he said with a slight growl. "Be still my heart."

She grimaced and said with mock severity, "That sounds a little nineteen-fifties, Bobby."

"It's Mr. Callahan." He grinned. "Maybe it does sound a bit old-fashioned, but it's a lost art."

"What exactly? Cooking? Or cooking for your man?"

He released her hand, and touched the brim of his hat. "Don't get me wrong. This goes both ways. Women don't have the time to take care of their men anymore, and the men won't take the time to please and care for their women."

Jane opened her mouth to reproach this statement, but she promptly shut it. He was right, she'd just never heard anyone say something quite like that. In fact, she'd never heard anyone speak the way he did—honest, forthright and just plain sexy.

"So you're a chef," he said, giving her another twirl. "Where do you work?"

"So, you didn't try and find out about me, huh?" she chided. But deep-down, she held her breath for his answer.

"As a matter of fact I did. But the Turnbolts didn't know a Jane Hefner." His eyes narrowed. "Did you crash that party or something?"

She laughed. No, the Turnbolts wouldn't have recognized her name. They'd only known her as an Al-Nayhal, and if Bobby had tried to describe her that might not have worked, either, as they'd only seen and spoken to her briefly. "The truth is, I'd heard who the guest speaker was going to be, and I just had to get in to see him, no matter what the danger."

He grinned. "Well, I'm flattered, darlin'."

If he wanted to, he could say *darlin'* at the end of every sentence.

"So you didn't tell me," he said, catching her attention, once again. "Where do you work, so I can come in and—"

"Heckle me?" she joked.

"Have a bite," he said slowly, his eyes hooded and

slightly dangerous as they swayed slow and easy into the strains of the music.

Ripples of excitement ran through her, and she knew she was powerless to resist this man. They had serious chemistry, the kind the women's magazines were always having you take a poll to help you find. "Unfortunately, I don't work at a restaurant here. I was working in California for a long time, but I've recently acquired some new family members here, and a quasi-catering gig." She shook her head. "It's a strange situation, and probably dull for you—"

"Stop right there." He laced his fingers with hers, stepped closer, even as the music ended and couples left the dance floor. "Dull is the very last thing you are."

"Jane?"

Jane heard her name being called, recognized the man who spoke it, but had a hell of a time turning away from Bobby to face him.

"I think we've interrupted something," Jane heard Rita say softly, but with a ring of a smile, behind her.

"And I am glad of that," Sakir said coldly. "Jane?"

This time Jane turned, saw her brother and sister-in-law standing there and smiled apologetically. Rita looked bright-eyed and interested. Sakir, on the other hand, appeared intense and irritated.

Unsure of what was bothering her brother, Jane made quick introductions. "Sakir, Rita, I'd like you to meet—"

Sakir cut her off. "We know each other."

"Oh," Rita said, confused.

"Unfortunately," Bobby muttered, from beside her.

Jane turned to look at Bobby Callahan. Gone was the

charming, funny and highly sensual man she'd just danced with, and in his place stood a man of stone, a thick vein pounding in his temple.

"What's wrong?" she whispered to him.

Bobby acted as though he hadn't heard her. He stared at Sakir, his gaze hooded like a predatory hawk.

"Is it possible for us to behave like civilized gentlemen tonight, Callahan?" Sakir said, ice threading his tone as he stuck out a hand in Bobby's direction.

Eyes narrowed, Bobby stared at Sakir. "It'll be a cold day in hell before I shake the hand of the man who stole my father's land and helped put him in the ground."

Three

It had been close to eight years since his father's death, yet the anger that now burned in Bobby's blood was stronger and more dangerous than ever.

His fierce gaze never left Sakir Al-Nayhal as they seemed to circle each other, challenging each other, without moving a muscle. The party went on around them. Guests ate and drank, women flirted with men and the host and hostess gave their tenth tour of the night.

Beside Bobby, Jane tugged at his hand and asked, her voice threaded with concern, "What in the world is going on?"

Gesturing to Sakir, Bobby muttered a terse, "This man, this friend of yours, is a thief and a liar."

"What?" said Jane in shocked tones. "What are you talking about?"

"A rich and powerful thief, but a thief nonetheless."

"Careful, Callahan," Sakir warned, his mouth grim with dislike.

"Sakir?" Al-Nayhal's wife spoke, her tone even, but concerned. "Maybe we should discuss this at another time? This doesn't seem like the place to—"

"Discuss what?" Jane demanded, this time looking at Sakir.

"He is angry because his father lost his family's land," Sakir explained to Jane.

"He didn't lose anything," Bobby growled with deep menace, not caring who overheard him. "You set out to destroy him, and you did."

"Destroy him?" Sakir repeated, sniffing as if that were the silliest idea in the world.

"How many times did you approach my father about buying his property, Al-Nayhal?"

"I will not go over this again—"

"What was it? Five, six times?"

"Sakir, what is he saying?" Jane demanded, alarm threading her tone now.

Sakir sighed with annoyance. "When I came to Texas I wanted to acquire several acres of land. The oil industry here was on the decline. Callahan's land was on the auction block, and in dire need of environmental changes I might add, so I acquired it."

Bobby snorted bitterly. "You're getting so good at spouting off that story, somebody'll think you actually believe it." His voice dropped, and through gritted teeth he uttered, "Bottom line is, my father wouldn't sell you his land, so you went about getting it any way you could."

"Rita's right," Jane said as people began to stare. "Maybe we should take this conversation inside."

"Or better yet, let us postpone the discussion altogether," Sakir suggested tightly. "It grows tiresome."

Bobby finally turned to look at Jane, who appeared pinched and uneasy. "How do you know this guy?" he asked her, not caring that she'd stepped back a few inches.

She didn't answer him at first, looked from him to Sakir, then back again.

"She is my sister," Sakir supplied for her.

"What?" A slow, sinking feeling pushed into Bobby's gut.

Sakir raised his already tipped chin. "She is Al-Nayhal."

"I told you that I had family here," Jane said slowly, her green gaze—so like her *brother's*—filled with worry.

But Bobby was in no mood to offer her any comfort. "You also said that your name was Hefner."

"It is. Sakir's my half-brother. I didn't know he existed until just a few months ago."

Bobby sniffed derisively. "I'm sorry for you."

Sakir spoke in a quiet, though ultra-threatening, tone. "Again, I caution you to be careful, Mr. Callahan."

"Or what?" Bobby spat. "You'll try and take the measly twenty-five acres of my father's land you left behind? Not going to happen. I've paid you every last cent for the place, including interest."

Sakir acknowledged this with a nod. "So you have." He placed a hand protectively around his wife's shoulders. "Understand, Mr. Callahan, that, like you, I feel impassioned over the well-being of my family."

Dark, blood-red heat tumbled through Bobby's chest and gut. He looked at Jane, at the beautiful, seductive woman who had captured his mind and body, had made him feel alive for the first time in a month, with new eyes. Was it possible that this whole thing had been nothing more than a game to her? Did she know about his history with the Al-Nayhals?

Bitterness flooded him. He had to remember that this woman belonged to a family who apparently thought it was nothing to use and hurt others—all in the name of acquisition.

"Jane is part of my family," Sakir continued ominously, in the same tone he'd used eight years previous to tell Bobby he'd never sell the Callahan's land back to a Callahan. "And I ask you not to forget that."

"Believe me, I won't," Bobby said without emotion before he turned and walked away.

When Jane sat down next to Rita at a nearby table a moment later, she felt as though she'd just been tossed into an emotional whirlpool. Bobby had stalked off in one direction and, when she'd tried to speak to Sakir to ask him a few questions, he'd taken off in the other direction, leaving Jane with bits and pieces of a cruel, wicked, time-worn story. The man she was desperately interested in getting to know on one side and her newly found brother on the other.

The dry heat from the barbecues moved over and through her, making her feel breathless and very weary. What in the world did she do now? Try to find out both sides of this tale? Or give up on a potential relationship, give up on something that seemed real—give up on a chance for something of her own? Because this thing between her and Bobby was tainted with her new life, a life she hadn't even come to grips with, much less embraced.

A deep longing for the familiar moved over her in smooth, uncomplicated waves. She knew it was a childish thought, but she missed her mother, missed how the woman had held her and kissed her hair when she felt unsure of the world.

"I'm so sorry about all of this, Jane." Beside her, Rita inched closer, her forced smile uneasy.

"What just happened?" Jane asked.

"That was pretty much business as usual for Sakir." Rita grimaced. "I only know Bobby by reputation, but that was a very different view of the charming cowboy I've heard the women around town go on about."

Very different from the man Jane had made love to ten days ago and flirted with tonight. "Do you know what really happened to his father's land?"

"Sakir's only talked about it once. Supposedly, Bobby's father made some foolish deal with a shady oil-drilling company. They never paid, and much of the land was ruined because of their bad drilling practices. Soon after, the property was seized by the bank and put on the auction block. Sakir was just getting started here. He wanted to buy some property for grazing land for cattle. There was nothing spiteful in the purchase, I don't think."

Mixed emotions flooded Jane as she listened to her sister-in-law. Bobby's loss and Sakir's gain. Nothing seemed right, but she wasn't certain of what was wrong or who was in the wrong. "Bobby accused Sakir of putting his father in the ground. What did that mean?"

Rita looked pained. "Bobby's father passed away just a few months after the land was sold."

"Oh, God." Jane could hardly make sense of all of this. Losing your land, then your father. Caring for your sister alone. Wasn't he entitled to some anger and hostility?

But was that anger misplaced?

She didn't know.

"Bobby also spoke about twenty-five acres?" Jane prompted.

Rita nodded. "Sakir did let Bobby buy back a few acres, along with the old house he'd grown up in."

"Why?"

"I don't know."

"And why not let him buy back the whole thing if he could?" Jane asked, as much to herself as to Rita.

Rita shook her head, played with a silver fork. "I honestly don't know. Sakir won't go into that, and I didn't want to push him. It's a sore subject."

"For them both." The heat from the barbecues was almost irritatingly suffocating now. "Why won't Sakir talk about this with me?"

"Sakir doesn't like his honor questioned."

Jane released a breath. Sakir was just like his eldest brother, Zayad, the Sultan of Emand. Business was done in a strict fashion, no games. But they were both very honorable, very good, kind men. She couldn't imagine Sakir doing something underhanded.

"By the way," Rita said with quiet familiarity. "How

do you know Bobby Callahan? You didn't just meet to-night, did you? You seemed…close."

Her sister-in-law's words ripped at her heart. They had been, in a crazy, short time, oddly connected. By a mutual desire, a steady interest and a similar pain. "We met at the Turnbolts' charity function."

"And?"

"And what?"

A soft, knowing smile touched Rita's lips.

Jane laughed half heartedly, shook her head. "You're very good at this."

Leaning in, Rita whispered, "I have a sister. Ava can never keep a secret from me, either."

Jane looked out over the crowd, tried to spot Bobby Callahan, but he was nowhere to be found. Odds were good that he'd already taken off. When Jane found Rita's gaze once again, she studied the woman. "How good is our friendship?"

A warm smile touched Rita's mouth. "Well, I'd say we're sisters now."

Jane nodded, then lowered her voice and said, "Bobby and I were together at the Turnbolts' charity do."

"Together?" Rita repeated.

Jane raised her brows suggestively.

"Oh," Rita said, surprised.

"It was one night, amazing, wonderful…" She put her head in her hands and groaned.

"I understand," Rita said comfortingly.

"Sakir can't know this," Jane said gravely.

"Sakir doesn't need to know this," Rita assured her. "It's your business, your relationship."

Jane looked up and heaved a sigh, tracing the edges of the white china plate before her. "Well, I think any chance of a relationship was just—"

"Tossed out the window?" Rita supplied.

Feeling overwhelmingly grievous, Jane shook her head. "Try catapulted."

He could go to hell for thoughts like this.

But as Bobby Callahan rode like the devil over his land, he felt defiantly resolute.

Finally, he would have his revenge on Sakir Al-Nayhal. Finally, he would honor the memory of his father.

On Josiah Callahan's deathbed, he'd asked just two things of his son, to take care of his sister, Kimmy, and to pay back the man who had stolen so much from them. There was nothing Bobby wouldn't do for his father, for the man who had felt honored to be the parent of a handicapped daughter, the man who had considered his life to be the easiest and most rewarding a man could have.

The part of Bobby that felt angry at his dad for giving up and leaving him and Kimmy alone, would forever be buried in his heart.

He hauled back the reins in his fist, brought his horse to a stop just inches from the property line he'd spent years memorizing. The line that separated his land from the land Sakir Al-Nayhal had stolen. For the first three years after his father's death, Bobby had sat on this imaginary line, his butt in the dirt, his heart and soul wrecked. He'd imagined all sorts of ways to get his revenge. He'd fantasized about getting even with Sakir Al-Nayhal. Making him pay, making him realize what pain really was.

The woman who'd called herself Jane Hefner entered his mind with a quick shot of desire. Bobby wasn't altogether sure if she'd lied to him or not, if she'd known who he was all along and had been playing him—after all, he wouldn't put anything past that family.

But he almost didn't care.

Jane Hefner Al-Nayhal was going to be the answer to his eight-year quest. She liked him, he knew it, and he was going to make her fall in love with him, desperately in love with him, then toss her back into the arms of her brother, rejected and shattered. Then her brother would see what it was like to watch someone he loved fall apart.

Sakir Al-Nayhal had destroyed Bobby's family.

Now Bobby was going to destroy Al-Nayhal's.

Four

Jane hadn't touched a drop of alcohol the night before. She hadn't danced into the wee hours with her heels in one hand and the palm of a gorgeous man in the other. And yet, she felt as though she was suffering the worst hangover of her life.

Was it possible to get drunk on confusion and disappointment?

Jane rolled to her back and faced the morning sun that slammed into her bedroom with ferocious intensity. Much like a spotlight, she mused glumly. She had come to Texas in hopes of redefining her future, but eleven days ago a major roadblock had been thrust out in front of her in the glorious shape of a six-foot-three cowboy. The truth of it was, she was still intrigued by him, attracted to him. She still liked him—a lot—despite the feud between him and her brother. But if she pursued her desires, regardless of what she'd heard and seen last night, would both Bobby and her brother reject her?

She closed her eyes and sighed. At this point, she realized dolefully, she couldn't decide whose rejection would pain her the most.

A soft knock at the door interrupted her thoughts, and she unfolded the covers and pushed her tired self out of bed as she called, "Come in."

Sakir and Rita's housekeeper, a very serious-looking woman in her mid-fifties entered the room, too perfectly starched and coifed for 8:00 a.m. She inclined her head. "Good morning, Miss Al-Nayhal."

Jane smiled at the older woman as she reached for her robe. "Good morning, Marian. Would you please call me Jane?"

"His Highness wouldn't like that."

Jane pulled the belt of her white robe with a little too much force. "We don't have to tell him."

The woman frowned deeply, and ignored Jane's comment. "You have a phone call, Miss."

Jane glanced over her shoulder, her gaze settling on the nightstand where she expected to see a telephone. But oddly, there wasn't one. She hadn't noticed this before, and thought it strange in an enormous house like this that guest rooms weren't equipped with phones.

Seeming to read her thoughts, Marian simply said, "Mrs. Al-Nayhal hasn't had time to install telephones in every room."

"Of course not," said Jane, feeling sheepish, her toes

sinking into the thick cream carpeting. "With the new baby and all."

Marian neither agreed nor disagreed with this. Instead she thrust the cordless phone at Jane, who took it from her with another quick, "Thank you."

After a pert nod, the older woman turned on her perfectly polished black shoes and left the room.

Wondering if whoever was calling her still remained on the line after all of that nonsense, Jane cradled the phone to her ear and said hopefully, "Hello?"

"Well, that was one helluva party last night, wasn't it?"

Her heart dropped into her stomach, and she actually felt herself beam with pleasure and relief. The rough timbre of his voice, edged with that slow charm made her smile, made her recall their first night together. She was surprised by the intense reaction, albeit a little worried about this undeniable need she had to hear his voice again.

"One helluva party?" she repeated with a trace of sarcasm. "I suppose. If you like a little conflict with your barbecue."

His chuckle lacked real mirth. "Yeah, well, we took things too far."

"You and Sakir, you mean?"

He paused, then sighed. "It's all water under the bridge now."

"Is it?" she asked in a small voice. The way Bobby had glared at Sakir last night suggested the opposite.

"It has to be. We both have to get over all this past BS." She could practically hear him shrug. "Well, I do anyway."

Not that she didn't want him to feel this magnanimous spirit, but she couldn't help wondering how, after such a display of hatred last night, he could make such a turnaround. "Why the sudden change of heart?"

"This feud is getting in the way of something real important."

"What's that?"

"Me asking you out."

Jane grinned gleefully, and snuggled her ear closer into the phone. This was an answer she liked. "Would it appear too desperate to say that I'm really glad you called?"

He laughed, and the sound was genuine this time, not forced. "No, darlin'. Sounds honest."

"Honest is good." The simple phrase was a mantra for Jane, had been ever since she could remember. Even as a child, her mother had always led her to believe that honesty was the only way to live her life. Painful or painfree. Ironic as her mother was holding onto a very deep secret regarding Jane's father during that time.

"Pick you up in an hour?"

Bobby's query shot her back into reality, and she muttered swiftly, "I'm sorry, what?"

"I said I'll come by, pick you up in an hour," he repeated.

She glanced at the clock, then down at her robe. "It's only eight o'clock."

"All right," he acquiesced with a trace of mock annoyance. "Two hours."

"So bossy," she chided playfully. "And would you like to tell me what to wear, as well, Mr. Callahan?"

His voice dropped to a husky whisper. "Damn right I would, but with the suggestion I'd make you might just get arrested the minute you step out your front door."

She laughed. "Casual elegant, it is then."

"Fine," he muttered dolefully.

"Are we really going to do this, Bobby? Are we really going to *date* after…well, after last week?"

"You bet. And we're going to do it the right way."

"The right way?"

"Hand-holding, then maybe a kiss or two…we're going slowly this time."

Little shots of thrill twirled in her belly, and she leaned closer to the phone, her lips brushing over the receiver, her mind conjuring images of that sweet, soft kiss. "Like courting?"

"Sure, but I won't be asking your brother for permission."

"No." His shot of cold humor put a slight damper on her romantic feeling, but she brushed it away.

"See you in an hour?"

"I thought you said two."

"I don't want to wait that long. Do you?"

"No." The excitement that ran a marathon through her blood mingled irritatingly with caution, brought on by last night, and her judgment and blind hope that he was trustworthy.

"Bye, darlin'"

"Bye." As Jane hung up the phone, slipped out of her robe and headed for the bathroom, she wondered what she was in for downstairs. She wondered if her brother would raise holy hell when he found out what she was doing.

But as soon as she stepped under the hot spray of the shower, she let her mind fall to more appealing queries, such as what delights awaited her on her first real date with Bobby Callahan.

Forty minutes later, down in Sakir's very masculine, very brown leather- and mahogany-paneled library, Jane got the answer to her first question.

Not *holy hell*, but definite displeasure.

"He is using you, Jane."

Dressed in a white kaftan, her brother looked impenetrable and uncompromising sitting behind his desk.

Jane stood before him wearing a pale-green sweater, white jeans and a determined set to her chin. "I don't think so, Sakir, but even if that were true, it's my choice to make."

"Rita has told me that she spoke to you regarding the history of Bobby Callahan and myself."

"Yes."

"The man will do anything to get back at me, including hurting the members of my family, I am certain of it." He leaned forward, lifted his brows. "He despises me that much."

"Does he have a right to?" The question fell from her mouth without thought, and she quickly added, "In the short time I've gotten to know you, I see a great man, an honorable, caring man. But we all do things that live in the gray. Was this deal with Callahan one of those moments?"

His mouth set in a thin line, Sakir uttered, "You ask your brother such a question?"

"I ask my brother for the truth, that's all." She sighed,

sat in the chair opposite him and laid a hand over his. "I'm a big girl, Sakir. I can handle the truth. Whatever it is."

The ire in his eyes and the tight expression of a businessman he wore, softened. "You will always receive the truth from me. Be assured of that."

She offered him a gentle smile. "Thank you."

He nodded, then exhaled heavily. "There was no maliciousness in the procurement of Bobby Callahan's land. After the drilling company left, the land was in a bad state. They had dug and torn the soil and spilled oil everywhere. It was an environmental nightmare. The elder Callahan could not care for, or repair, the property, and the bank was foreclosing. If it had not been I who made the purchase, it would have been someone else. And I have no doubt that buyer would not have been as generous in the end."

"You're talking about how you allowed Bobby to buy back a few acres of the land?"

"Correct. I am sorry about his father's death, but the anger he has for me is misplaced. And his unreasonable manner and quick anger make him dangerous."

"That's ridiculous," Jane tossed out, but in the back of her mind she couldn't help but wonder. Her stomach tightened with worry, and the reaction irritated her no end.

"You saw him last night," Sakir continued. "He was acting like a madman."

"He was angry, and he clearly holds a grudge the size of Texas against you. But a madman? No way."

"I will not allow you to walk into that fire, Jane."

She slipped her hand from his and laughed. "Allow me?"

It had been close to ten years since she'd heard words like that, and even then she'd rejected them. Most of the time. Coming from a man, a command such as this one really made her blood simmer. After all, she'd had no father, no male figure of authority in her life, and she wasn't looking for one now.

Leaning back in his chair, Sakir stared at her, his eyebrows set. "You must understand. You are Al-Nayhal. You are my sister, and I—" He broke off, looking rather embarrassed, but continued at any rate. "I have come to care for you a great deal."

An understanding smile nudged at the corner of her mouth. Clearly, it was far easier for her to show emotion than Sakir. "I love you, too, big brother."

"I do not want to see you hurt. Can you not understand this?"

"Of course."

"Then you will abide by my decision."

"No." She wasn't about to roll over and play the "little sister," no matter what judgments Sakir had made about Bobby's motives in asking her out.

"You are as stubborn as my wife," Sakir grumbled.

She laughed and stood. "Thank you. I take that as a compliment. Rita's wonderful."

"Yes."

"Listen, I've been making my own choices for ten years now, and I've done a pretty good job of it." She walked around his desk, leaned over and kissed his cheek. "Trust me, okay?"

His gaze found hers, and there was unabashed worry there. "It is Bobby Callahan I do not trust."

The doorbell rang just then, and Jane offered Sakir one last, faith-inducing smile before she turned her back on him and left the room.

If it were possible, Jane looked even more beautiful in a pair of form-fitting white jeans than she had in all that finery she'd worn the first night they'd met. Course, that could be just his taste, Bobby thought, shoving his truck into third as he shot up Hollyhock Drive. Sure, he liked dresses on a woman, but nothing could beat denim on curves.

Forcing his gaze onto the road and away from her slim thighs, he asked, "Have you had breakfast?"

"You hardly gave me time," she replied, a smile in her voice.

"Sorry about that."

"No, you're not."

He turned to her, grinned sinfully. "No, I'm not. I wanted to see you."

A slight pink blush crept up her neck, matching the haze around the morning sun before them. Bobby thought it was just about the sexiest sight he'd ever seen, and he wondered if he'd be able to pull this off—stay unaffected with this woman.

"So," she said, tugging him from his thoughts. "Where are we going?"

"A great place with real Texas ambiance and one helluva chef."

"Sounds good."

But when they turned into a driveway marked Private Property and drove through a set of weathered iron gates emblazoned with the letters *KC* Jane turned to him, her dark eyebrows raised. "What are the specials today, chef?"

He chuckled. "Bacon, eggs, maybe a slice or two of toast if I manage not to burn it."

Her gaze shifted to the landscape around his home. The pasture land, grazing horses, miles of sky above. No matter what the size of his property now, Bobby thought with a deep sense of melancholy, it was still home and it always felt right to be there.

She turned back to him. "Breakfast at your house. That's pretty intimate." Her full lips curved up at the corners. "And I thought we were taking things slow."

Bobby just grinned as he brought the truck to a dusty halt in front of his ranch house. The last thing he wanted with this woman was slow. Ever since they'd made love, he'd ached to touch her again, have her beneath him, on top of him, in front of him. But for his plan to come off, he needed to take his time, give her a little romance. Hell, he might even enjoy it.

He was quick to step out the driver's side and walk around the truck. He helped Jane out, then took her hand. "Well, I suppose I'd better admit it. I didn't bring you here *just* for breakfast."

Mock shock settled over her features. "No kidding."

"You implying I'm some kind of rogue cowboy?" Bobby asked lightly as they walked around the side of the house and down the stone pathway.

"I wouldn't dare."

Shifting the Stetson on his head, he laughed. "Well, it'd be the truth, on most days."

"But not today?"

"Today, I brought you here so you could see who I was. After last night, I don't think you got a pretty clear picture."

The air around them cooled, and Jane's voice dropped. "Maybe not."

She had reservations about him, he knew. And rightly so. It was also clear as river water that she was confused, not sure what he was about and what he was after.

Dammit.

Every time he looked into those dark-jade eyes of hers, Bobby had the same problem. He needed to keep his cool, stay in control of the situation and himself if he was going to finish this mess with the Al-Nayhals and get his father's ghost off his back once and for all.

"This." They reached the corral then, and Bobby released her hand and pointed into the ring. "This is who I am. This is why I cling tight to this land, and its past. Here's my passion, Jane."

With curious eyes, Bobby watched her take in the sight before her, then turned to see what she was seeing. While three children waited atop their horses, Abel helped sixteen-year-old Eli Harrison up the ramp and out of his wheelchair, then onto the back of Sweet Grace, a gray mare. Eli laughed and patted his horse, and while the other kids whooped and clapped excitedly around him, one of the ranch assistants belted Eli securely into place.

With a deep inhale, Jane turned her gaze from the corral and gave him a brilliant smile. "I'd like to meet them."

A shot of surprise registered in Bobby's gut, and he returned her smile. He hadn't expected her to say that.

Maybe how wonderful the place was or what great work he was doing—the usual thing women said when they stopped by the ranch. But as he'd suspected from the first night they'd met, Jane Hefner Al-Nayhal was far from the usual.

"How about after breakfast?" he asked, taking her hand again. "And after they finish their lesson?"

She squeezed his hand. "Okay."

With a wave to Abel, Bobby led Jane away from the corral, back down the path and through the yard. When they entered the house, Deacon, Abel's ancient dog, was asleep on the rug in the large kitchen. The spotted brown mutt barely raised his lids when they walked in.

Bobby motioned for her to have a seat at the nicked wood table over by the bay window. "Make yourself comfortable and I'll get to work in here."

"Weren't you the one who wanted the woman doing all the cooking in the kitchen?" Jane teased, sitting down at the table and smiling.

"That's not what I said and you know it."

Elbows on the table, chin resting on the back of her hand, she looked too comfortable in his house, at his kitchen table. "Okay, you said something like you appreciate it when a woman can cook."

"Damn right." He turned back to the counter and cracked a few eggs into a bowl, then grabbed a fork. "Just as you get to appreciate a man who can cook."

"Only if he doesn't burn the toast."

He tossed her a wicked glare, and she laughed.

"You sure you don't need any help?"

"I can make bacon and eggs with my eyes closed, darlin'."

She gave a soft whistle. "Now, that's something I'd like to see," she said, easing herself out of her chair and onto the floor, where she hunkered down next to the dog.

With a grand yawn, Deacon opened his eyes and rolled to his back, ready for a few scratches from the pretty lady who was visiting his bit of rug. The scene was a nice one—easy conversation as Bobby stirred eggs, Jane kissing Deacon's dusty face as she rubbed his pink belly. For just a moment, Bobby almost forgot the reason she was here.

Almost.

Ten minutes later, they were sitting across from each other at the table, eggs and bacon before them. Though she ate heartily, Jane kept glancing out the window at the yard and corral beyond. "Must be comforting to know your future."

The statement had Bobby pausing, a slice of toast poised at his lips. "What do you mean?"

She gestured around the kitchen. "You have this place, and a clear purpose. You know who you are and what you want and where you're going to be in ten years."

Bobby bit into the charred toast. He'd never thought of himself as set in his life, sure of his future. Maybe because he was so damn obsessed with the past. He caught her eye and raised an eyebrow. "You don't know what you want, Jane?"

"I thought I did."

"You're a member of a royal family now, you can probably do whatever you want."

"If we're talking about money, sure, but that's never where true happiness and fulfillment lie, is it?"

True happiness? Christ, he didn't know. He hadn't known true happiness since he was a kid, hanging out with his family, back when they were whole and happy. Bobby probably wouldn't know true happiness now if it rose up and bit him on the chin. And if it did, he'd push it away. He didn't deserve to feel good—not yet.

Jane continued, "The thing is, money and situation can't bring about purpose. That has to come from inside your gut." She placed her fork on her plate and sighed. "I thought opening my own restaurant was the be-all and end-all for me, but now I'm not so sure. What gets to me is that I was so sure of it before, back in California. The restaurant of my own, a family of my own some-day. That was my passion, what drove me. Then this man comes along and tells me he's my brother—that back when my mother worked in politics, she met a man and had a short-term affair with him, and that this man was my father. Oh, and right, he also happened to be the Sultan of Emand—"

"What?" Bobby prompted, watching her mouth drop into a apprehensive frown before his eyes. The sight bothered him far more than it should.

"Well," she said, shrugging. "I was sort of tossed into someone else's life—a life that would probably thrill most people. I mean, Emand is beautiful and the people are great and I want to *want* to be a part of them. But I found myself only feeling discontented there, and then guilty because of all the wonderful things my brothers have given me, offered to me. But, honestly, that life—their life—makes me uncomfortable. I've never been out in front, you know? Celebrity holds no appeal for me. I like simple. I like being behind the scenes."

"In the kitchen," he said, following her thought, though the mutual joke made her smile.

"Don't get me wrong, I'm glad I know the truth about where I come from, and having brothers is a gift, but my life doesn't seem to be my own anymore."

"Are your brothers making the decisions for you?" he said, his smile wavering as a thread of contempt lined his query.

Her large, almond-shaped eyes held understanding. "No, Bobby. There's no forcing me to do what I don't want to do. But I do feel obligated to try to be an Al-Nayhal. That's why I went to Emand, to experience the life and the culture, to learn as much as I could about my father and his family. And it was wonderful. But I felt like a tourist. I felt like I wanted to go home."

Bobby stared at her. Not since his parents were alive had there been such a conversation at his kitchen table. Most meals, he and Abel just talked about familiar things—the ranch, the food, the past, what had to be done the following day. On occasion a local politician's name would be tossed around, dragged through the mud, but that was about it. Never were there feelings and hopes and flowery stuff like that mentioned.

"Maybe you just want what every woman wants," Bobby pointed out, leaning back in his chair.

Her gaze moved over him in a slow, covetous way that made his chest and groin tighten simultaneously.

"What's that?" she asked.

"Security."

"In love or money?"

"In life."

She smiled then, a deep, warm smile that cut into his gut like a hot knife. "How did you get so insightful?" she asked.

"My sister probably," he said without giving it much thought. "Despite her disability, that girl had wisdom beyond her years. She always knew what was really important."

Kimmy had tried to make Bobby see what was important in life, too. But trying to teach a dead heart to beat again was an impossible task and he'd failed her time and time again in everything but the ranch.

Bobby stared into the green eyes of the woman who made his pulse shift erratically. In this, he wouldn't fail his sister or his father. Jane Hefner Al-Nayhal had complimented him on the direction he'd taken with his choices and his future. Little did she know that Bobby was attempting to navigate her future as well, but in a direction not nearly as successful.

Five

Sara, Eli, Daniel and May.

They were four of the most wonderful children Jane had ever met. Talking with them and hearing how much they enjoyed coming to KC Ranch made her heart twist with admiration for the man who had made it all possible.

Bobby Callahan was a few feet away, saying good-bye to May and her parents. The bright and beautiful teenage girl, who had lost her sight just ten months ago, was a new student at the ranch. Bobby's ranch foreman, Abel, had told Jane that the family traveled three hours each way to come to KC Ranch because of its reputation. He'd also told her that the girl had been completely closed down when she'd first arrived at the ranch. But the horses and the care of the staff had helped her crawl out of the dark place she was living in.

"Ready to go?" Bobby asked her.

Jane let her gaze travel over the sea of green and gravel, the trees and horses, and the sweet little ranch house that had felt warm and comfortable to a girl who regularly got lost in both the palace in Emand and Sakir's home outside of Paradise. "Not really, but I do have plans this afternoon."

"Another date?" Bobby asked casually, though the harsh grooves around his mouth hinted at his irritation at the thought.

A bolt of satisfaction knocked around in Jane's belly, and she wondered if he was going to make good on his promise and give her a kiss. He'd already held her hand, a kiss was the natural progression—even for a man bent on *slow moving*.

"Yes," she said seriously. "I do have a date. With my sister-in-law and a shopping mall."

His expression changed like quicksilver. Rigidity morphed into that lazy, roguish grin that made her knees buckle. He took her hand. "Let's go."

Jane waved goodbye to Abel and the kids and headed toward the truck with Bobby. On the way back to Sakir and Rita's house, Jane reflected on her time at KC Ranch and how she'd felt so alive there surrounded by the kids, air and life that was being nurtured every day. And once again, she thought how lucky Bobby was to have made such a valuable choice.

"The kids liked you."

Bobby's husky voice stole her from her thoughts, and she looked at him and smiled. "And I liked them. Maybe next time I can volunteer...maybe help out in the corral or make lunches or something."

"We welcome any and all help," he intoned seriously.

"You might regret saying that," she said sardonically rolling down her window for a shot of the sweet, early-fall wind. "You just might be seeing me every day."

"No regrets here," he said, his voice oddly gentle.

The hungry expression in his blue eyes made Jane's throat tighten, made her feel as though she couldn't swallow properly. She cleared her throat. "I had a great time today."

"Not disappointed in the humble surroundings?"

"Don't be silly," she admonished halfheartedly. "I'm a simple girl. I don't need fancy, never have—just clean and comfortable and homey."

His dark head tilted, his voice dropped. "Is that so?"

"That's so," she insisted. "Except…"

He frowned. "Except what?"

"The next time," she began as they turned into Sakir and Rita's long driveway, "why don't I make the toast?"

Bobby grinned suddenly. "I did warn you, darlin'."

The mall was fifteen minutes outside of Paradise. The massive lump of concrete consisted of two department stores, ten specialty shops and a small food court. Not exactly the ideal place to shop for elegant linens, china and flatware. Jane had suggested they travel to Dallas or rent what they needed, but Rita had assured her that she wanted the party to be as warm and rustic as it was stylish, and rented settings might feel too impersonal.

Jane had been more than happy to hear that Rita didn't want a stuffy affair, but as she combed through burgundy placemats that were made from a material she'd never heard of, she wondered if a happy medium were even possible here.

She tossed the items back onto the shelf and walked toward Rita, who was sitting on a bench holding Daya. Their faces were very close together and Rita was whispering something to her two-month old daughter. A combination of emotions swelled inside Jane—jealousy, affection, happiness, hope.

"How do you not eat her right up?" Jane said, coming to stand before them.

Rita kissed Daya. "I eat a large meal right before I pick her up to snuggle."

Jane laughed. "Is having a baby the best thing in the world?"

"Definitely. Of course, it helps having a husband."

"Yeah, and I bet Sakir changes her diapers," Jane said sardonically.

"Actually he does. And in the middle of the night, too."

"No way," Jane said, aghast. She couldn't imagine her stoic brother changing poopy diapers at one in the morning.

"Men are funny, aren't they?" Rita stood up, cuddled the baby against her chest. "They only let you see one side of them until they trust you."

As Jane helped her sister-in-law reorganize her stroller, shopping bags, diaper bag and blankets, she wondered if Bobby was only allowing her to see one side of him. She guessed he was. After all, they hadn't known each other very long. But that only led Jane to wonder what the other side of him looked like. Was it the angry, bitter man she'd seen the other night or some-one else?

"Let's walk, shall we?" Rita suggested.

"Sure. We could head over to Young's. I hear they have a wider selection and a china department. And on the way we can talk more about the menu."

As the baby cooed and shoppers around them grabbed for the deals of the day, Rita explained, "I want something fun and interesting. Same as the food. Can that be any broader?" She laughed at herself. "My sister, Ava, has made me promise to have ribs, so we have to have those."

Jane nodded. "I've never met your sister."

"Nope, not yet. Ava and her husband, Jared and their little girl, Lily, have been away, in Florida. Disney-world, actually." Ava rolled her eyes. "I can't even imag-ine Jared there, riding in teacups, standing next to Mickey for a photo op. Jared's great, but he's a pretty uptight guy."

Jane laughed. "Can't wait to meet them."

"You will. The whole gang will be at the party. Jared's grandmother, Muna, too. She's a trip."

They were just crossing the threshold into Young's department store when Rita spotted something in the distance and gave a little gasp. She turned to Jane and grinned widely. "We're being followed."

"What?"

"Well, actually, you're being followed." Rita poked her finger in the direction of women's nightgowns and lingerie. "Over there."

Jane looked in the direction that Rita indicated and

felt her heart drop into her shoes. That strange breath-lessness she'd felt when she'd first seen him at the Turn-bolts' party hit her again—and oddly just a few hours after she'd left him standing on her doorstep. Walking toward them, far too tall, dark and masculine to be shouldering through racks of white lace and silk, was Bobby Callahan. He was dressed in the same faded jeans, T-shirt, Stetson and boots, and he looked good enough to eat.

Bobby grinned at the two of them as he approached. "Afternoon, ladies."

Jane smiled brilliantly at him. "Afternoon, Mr. Callahan."

"How are you, Bobby?" Rita asked, a slight wariness threading her tone.

Bobby nodded. "Real good, thanks."

"Shopping for undergarments?" Jane asked, eyeing the row of silk and cotton he'd just emerged from.

"Don't wear undergarments." He winked at her, and when she blushed he laughed. He turned to Rita, saw her balancing the baby in one arm and a large shopping bag that hadn't been able to fit under the stroller in the other, and said immediately, "Let me help you with those, Mrs. Al-Nayhal."

"Thanks," Rita said, still sounding slightly uneasy, though she smiled pleasantly as he took the bag, then pushed the stroller through the store as they all walked along.

"So what are you shopping for?" Jane asked him, clearly wondering why he had come to search her out just hours after they'd seen each other.

"A new toaster."

At his grin, Jane laughed.

Bobby felt like the back end of an ass right now. He hated lying, especially as he stared straight into those bright-green eyes of Jane's, but his vow demanded that he use whatever means necessary to accomplish his goal. He knew that Sakir hated him, which probably meant that his wife felt less than fine with Bobby dating Jane. And Bobby needed to see Jane without any chance of interference. If Rita approved of him, helped Jane to cast aside any doubts about his sincerity, then they would have the time it took for a woman to fall in love. Just the thought of having Rita Al-Nayhal on his side, thinking him a good man—even telling her husband so—made a warlike smile break on his face.

"You missed me, didn't you?"

Jane's query ripped him away from his thoughts. When he raised his eyebrows to her teasing smile, she added, "It's okay to admit. It won't crush your masculinity."

Bobby chuckled. "I'm in a ladies' department store. I think my masculinity's already been compromised."

Beside them, Rita cuddled Daya and sang softly to her as Bobby continued, though he felt the woman's gaze on him from time to time. "Truth is, darlin', after I dropped you off, I realized that we hadn't decided what we're doing tonight."

"Doing tonight?" Jane repeated, rubbing her chin in mock thoughtfulness. "I don't recall—"

"Oh, c'mon, Jane," Bobby interrupted with an arrogant smile. "You know as well as I do that we're spending the night together." He turned to Rita then, gave her a wicked grin. "Pardon me, ma'am."

For a moment Bobby wondered if his take-what-you-want attitude offended Rita, but it didn't seem to. And after all, she *was* married to Sakir Al-Nayhal.

"No pardons necessary," Rita said at last, a cautious, though far more friendly smile tugging at her mouth. "This old married woman with a baby is gonna take off for a little bit. Be over here if you need me." She turned away from them and pushed the stroller over to the linens section.

A wave of triumph moved through Bobby. He'd made some headway here, made a few new and improved impressions that Rita would no doubt share with her husband. He turned back to Jane. She was smiling at him, familiar and open, with that touch of humor that made him want to kiss her and talk to her at the same time. Damn, why did he have to want her this way? Why couldn't she have been anybody but who she was?

"Something you wanna ask me, cowboy?" she teased.

"How about dinner tonight, maybe a moonlit ride?"

"I'm not the greatest horsewoman."

"You'll be fine," he insisted.

"How can you be so sure?"

"Because," he said, moving closer to her, his voice dropping to a husky whisper. "I'm going to teach you how to ride."

Jane felt her skin turn hot with his blatant innuendo. Here they were, standing in the middle of a crowded store with sales people pushing half-price sweaters, laughter and cries emerging from the many baby strollers around them, and all Jane could think about was lying horizontal on something moderately soft, with Bobby's mouth on hers.

"Come with me now," he murmured, his eyes liquid and hot.

The push to say yes was almost torturous, but Jane forced herself to decline. "I can't," she explained with a soft smile. "We're not finished here. I've got to work on this party. We have china and linens to buy today. This gathering is really important for my family, but most of all, it's important to my niece. It's her special day."

He looked thoughtful for a moment, then nodded. "I can wait."

Those words curled inside her, and the wicked smile he shot her only added fuel to an already blazing fire. It was a good thing Rita walked over then, because Jane was tempted to forgo the soft place to fall and kiss him rather obscenely against a rack of maroon table runners.

Little Daya was fussing, scrunching her face up and squirming in Rita's arms. Rita shrugged. "She's a little cranky. I'm thinking maybe we should go."

Jane glanced at Bobby. It would have been the perfect opportunity for him to get his wish. Baby crying, baby and mommy go home, Jane and Bobby start date right now.

But instead of waiting for the inevitable wail from Daya, Bobby said, "Let me try, Rita."

Jane gaped at him, so did Rita. It was a pretty well-known fact that men normally ran from a fussing baby unless they were biologically linked to the child.

"Are you sure, Bobby?" Rita asked, looking totally convinced that he was wasting his time.

He nodded and reached for Daya. "Trust me," he said confidently, wrapping the fussy little girl in his arms and tucking her against his massive chest. "I'll have her cooing in no time. Babies love me."

For a moment, Jane actually thought Daya was going to smile, but the flicker she saw on either side of the baby's mouth was step one of a full-on freak-out. As Bobby rocked her gently, Daya began to cry. When he tried making "shushing" sounds, Daya's cries turned to wails. And when he stopped moving altogether, a sound so painful and pitiful exploded from the little girl that both Jane and Rita reached for her.

Bobby looked dumbstruck as he handed the baby back to Rita. He kept on repeating the words, "I don't get it," over and over.

"It's all right, Bobby," Rita said over Daya's slowly deflating din, her gaze as concerned for him as for her daughter. "She's a little skittish with new people." Rita turned to Jane and rolled her eyes. "Just like Sakir."

Jane shifted her gaze to Bobby, who appeared a little detached, though he still had that crestfallen expression in his eyes. "Hey," she began, tucking her arm through his. "We need a big strong man to help us to the car. You up for it?"

"And you're bigger than most, Bobby," Rita said encouragingly, Daya now sans tears in her arms.

"No, you're the biggest," Jane amended, and the two women smiled at him affectionately.

Releasing a breath, Bobby shrugged. "All the compliments in the world can't make up for being rejected by a two-month-old, but I suppose I'll just have to take what I can get."

Jane smiled at him as he gathered the packages. Poor guy, she mused as she followed him and Rita out of the department store and into the parking lot. She knew it was a ridiculous notion, but she couldn't help wondering if the animosity Sakir had for Bobby might have somehow infected his daughter.

"Do you wish to torment me, my love?"

"Always," Rita said lovingly, sitting in her husband's lap, her arms around his neck.

Sakir pushed the leather captain's chair away from his desk and around to face the office's floor-to-ceiling windows. Holding his wife tightly, he looked out at the unending land of his backyard. "So, Callahan shows up at the shops, and you allow him to hold our child?"

"Yes."

"Why?" He eased her away a few inches so that he could look into her eyes. "You know how I feel about the man."

"And I know how Jane feels about the man," Rita said, strength in her tone. "And how he feels about her."

Sakir shook his head. "He is toying with her."

"I don't think so."

"What makes you so certain?"

Her hands cupped his face. The sun, hanging low in the horizon, bathed his handsome face in a reddish glow. "I know what need and longing look like in a man's eyes."

A slow grin worked its way to Sakir's face. "Yes, it would seem you do, dearest."

She leaned in and kissed him, warm and slow. "We had our struggles, too, Sakir," she said against his mouth. "But we overcame them and look at us now. Happy, in love, our beautiful child sleeping upstairs."

"Yes. I am a most fortunate man. I am proud of what we are and what we have. But Jane is my family now, too. She is Al-Nayhal."

"Jane is a strong woman with a great head on her shoulders."

"She will always be my little sister, dearest, and I would die before I let anyone hurt her."

"I know." Rita wrapped her arms around him, kissed him deeply, passionately. "That's why I love you so much."

"And I love you." His mouth covered hers hard then, his hands fisted her sweater.

"What can I do to take your mind off this?" she asked against his mouth.

"Off what?" he muttered, lifting her up and placing her on his desk. A sinful smile tugged at his mouth as he eased her back and lifted her skirt.

Six

"What's the big idea?"

The playfully gruff tone of voice made Jane grin. Poised at the stove, towel over her shoulder, she glanced over at Bobby, who was wearing a sexy pair of black jeans, a white shirt and a bewitching scowl on his handsome face. "Is there some problem, Mr. Callahan?"

"Yes." He crossed his arms over his chest and nodded at the steaming pan of chicken marsala she was working on. "Here I thought my eggs and bacon—"

"And toast," she teased. "Don't forget about the toast."

He rolled his eyes. "And my slightly charred toast…"

She laughed.

"Well," he muttered darkly, "I thought my meal was pretty damn impressive."

"It was," she assured him, turning back to the stove.

"But look at this." He gestured to the steaming pan of chicken and mushrooms in a wine and butter sauce. "It looks…professional."

"I did happen to mention that I am a chef, right?"

"Well, sure, but you didn't say what a big show-off you are."

She turned to glare at him, even tried to look shocked, but the sexy twinkle in his eyes had her busting out laughing again. "You won't care when you taste this, along with the penne and pine nuts."

"What, no dessert?" he said sullenly.

"I saw that ice cream in your freezer, Callahan. Ice cream trumps all other desserts, even the fancy ones."

He tossed a stray mushroom into his mouth. "I didn't know that."

"It's a chef thing." The late-afternoon sun settled over the house, bathing the spacious kitchen in a friendly, yellow light. "You know, some of my fellow chefs back in California actually prefer a hot dog with the works to sea bass and pesto butter."

"Yeah, well, who wouldn't?" Fork in hand, he stabbed a tender piece of chicken and popped it into his mouth. He groaned, and tossed her a hungry look. "I don't want this to sound sexist, but damn, lady, your place *is* in the kitchen."

Feeling incredibly close to him in that moment, she smiled a little shyly. "Thank you. I think."

Upon Bobby's insistence, and the fact that they were both starved and didn't want to wait until the food was plated, they stood side by side at the stove, eating chicken marsala and penne with pine nuts right out of their respective pans. As a chef, it was a fairly normal thing to do—skip the table and just go for the good stuff. But she'd certainly never tried it with a man before.

And such a man.

Bobby made no secret about his feelings—well, for her food anyway. He ate with gusto, showering her with praise after every bite. Pleasure coursed through her at his words and his passionate expression. This was why she'd gotten into culinary arts in the first place. Good food for people who really enjoyed it.

When Bobby'd had enough, he leaned against the counter and raised a brow at her. "You're amazing."

She flushed happily. "I'm glad you enjoyed it."

"I'm enjoying a few things lately." He gave her a wink. "You ready for a ride?"

Her breath caught in her throat as a mental image popped into her head that had nothing whatsoever to do with horses.

"Only take a minute to saddle up a couple of ponies." He pushed away from the counter.

And just as quickly, the sensual image faded. She had to bite her lip to stop herself from laughing. She really was growing desperate. Sad but true. She wanted to know when that kiss was coming—wanted to know why they had to take things slow when they'd started out so gloriously fast. She hoped he wasn't playing with her….

Sakir's warning was always there, under the surface of her skin, making her second-guess herself and Bobby.

"C'mon," he said, taking her hand and leading her

away from the kitchen and toward the front door. "The sunset can be real shocking it's so pretty."

"But we just ate," she warned, humor lacing her tone.

He chuckled. "It's not like swimming, Jane."

Any thread of worry she'd had disappeared and she laughed with him. "All right, lead on, cowboy. Into the barn and onto the back of the oldest and slowest horse you got."

A man and his horse were a sacred thing.

Bobby Callahan had always ridden solo. It was sort of a rule he had. No females behind him or in front of him. But tonight he had a woman sitting behind him, her arms wrapped around his waist, tight and warm, her thighs pressed against his, and she felt damn good. Lucky for him, Jane hadn't felt all that comfortable on Frankie, the horse he'd originally picked out for her, and Bobby wasn't about to walk the whole property alongside Ol' Dolly Parton, an aging blond mare who walked as though she were stepping in and out of a bucket of molasses, so he'd suggested riding double.

Beneath him, his gray stallion, Rip, tore up the ground while his gait remained as smooth as an ocean wave. The Texas landscape whizzed past, the air growing cooler with every dip of the sun into the horizon.

When Bobby had reached his destination, he slowed and let the stallion walk. "The sun's falling fast."

From behind him came a sigh, then the words, "It's beautiful."

"The land or the sunset?"

"Yes," she replied, a smile in her tone.

He chuckled. "Careful. Or you'll get bit."

"Bit by what?"

"The Texas bug."

"Oh, that."

"Think you could live here?"

The question was a basic one, simple actually when they were discussing sunsets and pretty scenery, their mood light and humorous. But the question also held a dot of intimacy that made Bobby real uncomfortable. Things were hopping around in his mind as of late, poking at his heart and gut over this woman. He liked her, liked her mind, her up-front way of talking. He was over the moon for her cooking, and those full lips and long legs....

Sweat broke out on his neck.

He had to keep reminding himself why he was pursuing her or there would be some real trouble ahead.

"Texas is already growing on me, Bobby. For many reasons." Jane shifted against him, her arms loosening slightly. "But in the end, I believe the place picks the person."

He snorted. "That's a bunch of bull, you know."

She laughed, let her head drop against his back. "Yeah, I know, but with a philosophy like that I don't have to make any decisions for myself."

"Looking for someone to make decisions for you, are you?" He hated the race of thrill and tension that snaked through him. And before she could answer him, Bobby twisted to the right, scooped her up and planted her in front of him on the horse.

Another rule broken, he mused. But hell, it was all

in the name of revenge, wasn't it? The darkly sarcastic thought made his gut twist, as did the hot look she sent him.

Her eyebrow arched over her left eye. "Is this standard horse protocol, Mr. Callahan?"

"No, but I wanted you in front of me, and instead of asking, I thought I'd make the decision for you." He kicked the horse forward into an easy walk.

With a grin, she wrapped one leg over his and inched herself closer. "So we're just going to keep riding this way?"

"Nope, we'll stop at that tree and turn around."

"Why?" She glanced over her shoulder, saw the massive tree, then turned back and curled into his chest. "Amazingly, I'm really enjoying this. I'd like to go farther."

"We can't."

Emotions were shooting off inside him like out-of-control firecrackers. With the center of her snuggled into him, fitting him perfectly, he wanted her, any way he could get her. Desire warred with an irritating wash of chivalry. He could feel her heart pounding against his chest. Was she excited, was she nervous? He wanted to protect her. But how did he protect her from himself?

She looked up. "Why can't we go farther?"

"Beyond that tree…" The words weren't as easy to speak as they were to think.

"What?" she asked, concern etching her features.

"That's your brother's land, darlin'."

For a moment, she just stared at him, then she nodded. "But I'm sure he wouldn't mind us—"

"I mind," Bobby said firmly, his gut tight now. "I've

never passed this boundary since the day the land was sold, and I don't intend to trespass now."

He brought the horse to a stop beneath the tree. They sat there, Rip shifting his weight beneath them. Bobby stared up at the massive trunk and pale-yellow leaves as though it was something to revile, wondering, as he always did, just how long it would take him to chop it down.

Jane's soft voice cut through his black thoughts. "Bobby, I've heard one side of this story. I'm smart enough to know that there's a lot more to it than just one side."

"'Course there is."

"You want to tell me?"

Bobby stilled. Sure, he wanted to tell her, every last bit. From his father's phone call telling Bobby in a miserable voice that Callahan land no longer belonged to the Callahans, to Bobby's nightly agony over a promise he wished he'd never made. But he couldn't say anything about that last bit, could he? Just like he couldn't change what was promised. He'd made the vow, and what he said here would need to work in his favor with regards to wooing Jane Hefner Al-Nayhal.

"You had to come home, right?" she prompted, "Leave your work when your father…"

"Had his land ripped from him?" Bobby finished for her. "That's right. Working the rodeo circuit was the best life a young man could know, but Dad needed the help. He was starting to really lose it. And with Kimmy… well, they both needed me."

"So you put your own life aside for your family."

He sniffed. "It's not as benevolent as it sounds, I promise you."

"Sounds like a sacrifice to me."

Admiration lit her eyes, and the sweet, honest smile she gave him nearly undid him. Why couldn't she have been a cold, unfeeling liar like her brother?

He looked away, looked deep into the land that would never again be his and begged to feel the comforting wave of anger. "Family takes care of family, simple as that."

"This whole thing sounds anything but simple." The wind blew over them, and Bobby tightened his hold on her. She released a weighty breath. "Have you ever thought about going back to the rodeo circuit?"

"My life is here now," he answered, his voice ripe with an acceptance he'd come to terms with long ago.

"And you never regret the sacrifice you made?"

"Hell, no." He didn't altogether believe the bold statement himself. Sure, he missed the circuit, the traveling. "How did we get on this subject? I thought you wanted to hear how your brother swooped in like a ravenous hawk and snatched up my father's land. You know, this property had been in the family for over fifty years."

"Did your father have to sell the land?"

"Yes," he said through gritted teeth.

"Why?"

"Made some deal with a seedy oil company." One that Bobby had always thought might have connections with Sakir Al-Nayhal, though he could never prove it.

"So Sakir didn't actually steal the land, he—"

Bobby interrupted caustically, "He tried to buy this land several times and my father told him to get lost. Your brother was proud and pissed off when he was rejected, and first chance he got, he took what he wanted."

She pushed away from his rigid body. "Why do you think he wanted this land so badly?"

Bobby shrugged, gave a derisive snort. "He said the land had major environmental issues that needed to be addressed."

"And that wasn't true?"

What was the point of this? Bobby thought angrily. With all the questions? It was like a damn inquisition. She was following a path that made Al-Nayhal look innocent, and Bobby wasn't going there with her. "It's getting dark, and so's my mood."

Her face was filled with contrition. "I'm sorry, Bobby. I just want to get to the truth."

"Why? Why do you care?" And didn't she know that the truth had many sides to it? Hell, if he really looked at the truth, turned away from supposition and what he believed in his heart, he might not be so quick to keep his word to his father.

"I care because I like you." She bit her lip, but didn't look nervous, just desperate to understand. "And you hate my brother. That's a problem for me."

"Yeah, I get that."

"I'm trying to build a bridge here."

As Rip shifted beneath them, his muscular body ready to fly again after the short rest, Bobby snaked his hand behind her neck and pulled her to him. His kiss was hard and unyielding. When he eased back, he found her gaze and said in a hushed, though ultra-serious whisper, "Sakir Al-Nayhal and I will never be friends. No matter how close you and I get, that fact will never change. Understand?"

Tipping up her chin, she nodded. "Yes."

"Can you handle that?"

"I don't know."

His hand tightened possessively around her neck. He wanted to kiss her again, nip her lower lip with his teeth—brand her somehow before he was forced to give her back to her brother. But the rabid hunger he felt worried him, and he released her, lifted her up and placed her behind him once again.

"Put your arm around me, Jane," he commanded.

Seconds after she wrapped her arms about his waist, he led Rip into a half turn, then kicked the gray stallion into a heart-jolting gallop toward the ranch house.

The sky had turned an eggplant color as the sun disappeared completely, giving in to the black night.

Jane sat beside Bobby on a white porch swing, a heavy quilt over their legs as they dipped spoons into a bowl of ice cream that Bobby held in his fist. Jane ate the sweet chocolate slowly, thinking about the passion that ran between her and Bobby. Not a romantic passion, but heat and walled-up anger and a need for redemption.

This relationship, if she could even call it that, was growing dangerous with every moment they spent together. Bobby clearly was swimming in a sea of bitterness. He turned away from the realities of his past, clung to his own beliefs. For what reason, she wasn't sure. But she feared she had a weakness for men with injured souls, men who loved her cooking and made her laugh. She suspected that in some way her brother had it right. Bobby Callahan could very well break her heart. And what a fool she was for taking that chance.

Her gaze flew to his face. So rough, so sexy, with eyes that held a thousand emotions, five hundred of which were happiness and hopefulness and caring for others and a deep sense of compassion. She wondered if the truth would ever set his soul free.

She took another bite of ice cream and said thoughtfully, "Romeo and Juliet."

Bobby turned to stare at her, eyebrows raised. "Pardon?"

"That's what's happening here. With us. Did you read that play in high school?"

"Sure. Boy and girl fall in love, then off themselves."

She grinned, pointed her cleaned spoon at his chest. "They *off* themselves, as you so delicately put it, because their families are bitter enemies and they'll never allow Romeo and Juliet to be together."

"I don't have any family, darlin'."

"It's the principle of the thing," she explained.

"So, what's your point? That we're going to end up dead if we continue to see each other?"

She laughed. "No, of course not." The laughter melted into a reluctant smile. "But we might end up hurt."

His expression changed from playful to cryptic in a nanosecond. "Anything's possible, I suppose. Found that out a long time ago." He dug his spoon into the frozen treat. "But…"

"But what?"

His gaze found hers. "Is the possibility of pain later on worth the pleasure now?"

"Wow, that's a question."

"All I'm saying is that we've got something here, happening between us. Why worry about the future?"

With her spoon mining into the ice cream, Jane replied, "Well, I guess because I'm a woman and that's what we do. Worry. About the future and a hundred other things."

Bobby set the bowl on the table beside the swing and pulled Jane onto his lap. "I think about you too damn much, you know?"

"I don't know if I'd put it that way, but I think about you, too."

"Yeah?"

"Yeah," she replied, grinning, allowing the heaviness of their ride and all conversation about family to fall away.

Bobby repositioned the blanket over her shoulders and let it cover him. "What do you think about?"

She smiled. "That night."

"Ah, yes. That night."

"Your eyes," she whispered.

He found her neck, grazed his lips over her pulse point, and uttered, "Your skin…"

She smiled, closed her eyes. "Your mouth…"

He pulled her face down to his and covered her mouth. This time, there was no anger in his kiss, only desire. He tasted like chocolate and cold, and the sound of his breathing, heavy and hungry, made every nerve in her body jump with excitement. When his tongue darted out, lapped at her upper lip, she opened for him, her breasts tightening in response. Such a heady reaction to just a kiss was new for her.

With a hungry whimper, she curled her arms around his neck and pulled his head closer so their kiss could go deeper. Running on pure instinct, Jane closed her lips around his tongue and sucked.

Bobby went stiff, then shuddered. He pulled away from her, and she saw that his eyes were near-black with need, his breathing labored.

"Did I hurt you?" she asked, concerned.

"Not yet, Juliet."

A strange blow of emotion sank into her chest. Why would he be the one to say that? To pull away and say something like that? He wasn't the one taking the chance here...was he? He was the one who didn't want to worry about the future. She closed her eyes for a moment, deeply confused, desire and frustration running a race in her blood.

He gently lifted her off him. "I'll take you home now."

"I didn't ask you to."

"I know." He took her hand and led her off the porch.

Seven

When Jane walked through her brother's front door that night, she felt weary, aroused and more confused than ever. What had started out as a light affair had shifted into something far more than casual fun. Bobby seemed to be agonizing over moments of intimacy, limited though they were, and Jane couldn't figure out why. Was it that he really didn't want her? Had that one amazing night they'd shared taken all the mystery out of their relationship?

Melancholy twisted around her heart. She felt the exact opposite. That one night had been an awakening for her, a moment where she'd come to realize that there might be a man out there for her—and the thought of exploring more nights in his arms made her breathless with anticipation.

As she walked into the living room, she felt a heavy gloom cover her, then noticed that it was the house that had brought on the feeling. Sakir and Rita's home was unusually quiet and dark for nine o'clock. No Marian, no Rasan, Sakir's assistant. Had everyone gone to bed? she wondered, following a dimly-lit hallway toward the kitchen. A nice cup of hot chocolate sounded like just the thing to take up to her room to aid her as she tried to get Bobby Callahan's blue eyes and hard mouth out of her head.

But before she reached the kitchen, a chunk of yellow light purged into the hallway ahead. Soft laughter followed. Both light and sound were coming from Sakir's library. There was something in the sound that drew Jane toward it like a tired body to a soft bed. She paused in the doorway, found Sakir and Rita sitting hand in hand on a brown leather couch. They were chatting with someone Jane couldn't see due to a white-leather high-back chair.

Sakir looked up when Jane entered the room and seemed to fight between a welcoming smile and a worried gaze. Jane wanted to tell him irritably that he didn't need to worry—that Bobby Callahan had barely touched her tonight, but she didn't get the chance when he quickly said, "You have a visitor. And a very charming one."

Rita nodded to the person before her, and Jane, eyebrows furrowed, stepped farther into the room. Rounding the chair, she nearly fainted with pleasure when she saw the beautiful, long-legged blonde.

"Mom!" she exclaimed, running straight for her like a lost toddler.

Crushed in her daughter's zealous embrace, Tara Hefner laughed. "How are you, sweetie?"

"I'm fine. But why didn't you call to tell me you were coming early? You weren't supposed to be here for another week."

"I wanted to surprise you."

Sakir nodded deferentially. "And a very welcome surprise it is."

Rita smiled in agreement.

Jane appreciated her brother and sister-in-law's kind welcome. She'd expected Sakir to be aloof, like their brother Zayad, maybe even a little cynical upon meeting the woman who'd long ago had an affair with his father. But if he felt anything at all on that front, he masked it very well.

"I've missed you so much," Jane said with undisguised passion.

"And I've missed you," Tara said, easing her daughter onto her lap. The blind woman let her fingers loose on Jane's face. "You feel tense. What's going on? Are you all right?"

The fact that her mother could feel her mood always unnerved Jane. Even after her mother had lost her sight, Jane had never been able to get away with anything.

Tara took Jane's hand and squeezed it. "Mr. Al-Nayhal was just telling me that you were out with a man who might not be the best company."

Jane tossed Sakir a semi-irritated glare. "Don't listen to my big brother, Mom. He's just being over-protective."

Rita laughed. "I'm afraid you're going to have to get used to that, Jane."

An eyebrow lifted in Jane's direction, Sakir shrugged lightly. "I merely was telling your mother the truth. And please, Tara, I wish for you to call me Sakir. We are family now."

Tara looked toward him, her unseeing eyes bright. "Thank you. It's good to have family."

"Sometimes," Jane said with a dry smile.

Everyone laughed, except Sakir, who managed a tight grin. For the next forty-five minutes, they sipped wine and talked about Jane's time in Emand, little Daya's entrance into the world and her upcoming party. When the clock in Sakir's library struck ten, Jane noticed her mother's well-disguised yawn.

"Are you tired?" Jane asked. "You had a long trip."

Tara nodded. "I am tired."

"I'll take you up," Rita offered kindly.

But Jane was already helping her mother to her feet. "No, thanks, Rita. I'll go with her."

"Your bags have been taken to your room," Sakir said, then turned to Jane. "Tara is in the blue room, just down the hall from you, yes?"

Jane nodded.

"Goodnight, Tara," Rita said warmly.

Her arm through her mother's, Jane guided the older woman upstairs. They walked several hallways chatting softly about the size of Rita and Sakir's home, and how they could have fitted their entire house inside the main hall.

The blue room was large and comfortable and, true

to its name, had bed linens, pillows and walls done in different shades of blue. The first thing that Tara wanted to do was unpack, but, as Jane had expected, her clothes and personal effects had already been put away.

With an easy sigh, Tara sat on the bed, her back resting against the headboard, and gestured for her daughter. "Come here, sweetie."

Feeling six years old, Jane crawled onto the bed and curled up beside her mother. She smelled like lavender and vanilla, and Jane let her head fall into the woman's lap.

"Now, tell me what's going on," Tara pressed gently.

Jane told her mom about her dates with Bobby Callahan, naturally omitting the night they'd shared at the Turnbolts' charity event. Then she went on to explain the situation between Sakir and Bobby.

Tara took a moment before answering, but when she did her voice was soft and wise. "It seems that neither Sakir nor Bobby is in the wrong here."

"I know."

"Bobby's story is a hard one. That's a lot for one soul to bear in a lifetime."

"And he hides the pain well."

"Through bitterness and a good defense?"

Jane looked up, surprised. "Yes."

"Well, that's a natural response to happiness or pleasure or anything good that happens."

"Why?" Jane asked.

Tara shook her head and said almost wistfully, "You feel guilty enjoying life when your other family members can't." Lovingly, she kissed Jane's forehead. "Don't you remember when we went to the beach for the first time after I'd lost my sight? Don't you remember how you felt?"

Undeserving, guilty. Yes, Tara was right. "Well, I don't know if it's anger or guilt that he feels, but whatever it is, it drives him." Jane sat up, took her mother's hands. "I really like him, Mom, but I can't help wondering if Sakir's right. Is Bobby Callahan out for more than just a few dates?" With her thoughts running over the night's events, Jane shrugged. "Maybe it's better if I just stay away from him."

Tara smiled. "Only you can make that choice."

"What would you do?"

"Oh, sweetie," Tara said on a laugh. "I couldn't make that call. I'm in the same boat as Bobby Callahan, still steeped in bitterness."

"What?" Jane stared at her mother. "That's not true."

"Like your friend, I hide it well. Perhaps better than most." Tara eased Jane's head back down to her lap. "But unlike your friend, I think I'm too old to change that part of myself."

Her mother's words settled over Jane, making her feel more confused and on edge than she had when she'd entered the house earlier that night. The admission from her mother was bizarre. Jane had never imagined Tara pining and wallowing over her affliction. Jane had only seen her strong, and spouting off wise words about survival and acceptance.

Good Lord, if her mother could fool her so, what should she think about Bobby Callahan? Would he ever change? Could he let go of his bitterness and embrace life? Did he even want to?

Jane couldn't help but wonder if she was seeing things, people clearly anymore—or through some rosy filter of her own making.

"Well," Jane began to say tightly, "it seems that I'm falling hard for a man who I'm fairly convinced can never offer me a future."

"It's strange," said Tara in an emotional voice. "Strange that our lives should follow such a similar path."

"What do you mean?"

"I, too, fell in love with a man who couldn't give me a future.

Sakir and Zayad's father. Yes, he'd been married, the leader of a country. Totally unavailable.

"But I have no regrets," Tara said, leaning down and giving her daughter another kiss on the forehead. "After all, he did give me you."

"You call that girl of yours. Tell her to get herself out here."

Bobby ignored Abel's ridiculous demand as he helped Laura Parker with her riding helmet. It was close to eight o'clock in the morning, the sun was shining brightly, and Bobby had an excited group of riders ready and waiting. For the first time since he'd taken Jane home last night, his mind wasn't on her.

But thanks to Abel, she was back to the forefront.

"Said she wanted to help, didn't she?" Abel persisted.

"She did," Bobby muttered.

"Well, we're going to need it later on today. Twice as many students as usual."

"We can handle things just fine."

"Don't be stupid."

Bobby threw the older man a dangerous glare. "She wouldn't come anyway. Something tells me she doesn't want to see me today."

"Why's that? What did you do?"

"What I always do." He'd found a reason to distance himself from any feeling that wasn't productive. He could handle anger or irritation or despair—even plain and simple sexual pleasure—but forging a connection between his black heart and another's strong, healthy one had him backing off to get his bearings, and once again reaffirm what he was doing with her. Damn, why couldn't he and Jane have stopped this the night he'd found out who she was? Bobby cussed under his breath as the reason stabbed at him. He hadn't stopped this tryst with Jane because he had payback on his mind.

Thing was, he hadn't bargained on liking the woman—wanting her, yes, but liking her, no.

The mare beside Abel shifted and stepped on the edge of the old man's foot. Abel swore darkly, then looked sheepish as the teenager he was helping brush down the horse lifted his eyebrows. He lowered his voice and leaned into Bobby. "You're going to end up a lonely old goat."

"Look who's talking," Bobby shot back.

The teenage boy chuckled, then stopped when Abel sent him a testy glare. Again, he leaned into Bobby and whispered, "That wasn't my choice and you damn well know it."

Bobby swatted at a fly. "Fine."

"But you do have a choice, boy."

Bobby looked Abel straight in the eye, prepared to utter some stay-out-of-my-business comment. The older man had been with Bobby for too long. He knew too much, spoke whatever was on his mind with little thought of the impact. But Abel also had been a good friend, so Bobby curbed the need to argue and muttered a quick, "I don't have time for this. As you said, we have a big group today," then walked away.

"Are you sure it's all right if I tag along?"

"Of course," Jane assured her mother as she pulled one of Sakir's cars into the driveway of KC Ranch. "Bobby's foreman said he'd love another set of hands helping the kids with their gear and lining them up and things like that."

"Because I don't want to be a burden."

The warm morning sun filtered through the passenger-side window, setting her mother's pretty face in a flattering pale-yellow glow. "Mom, why are you talking like this? It's not like you to be so—"

"Self-pitying? I know." Tara laughed weakly. "I'm feeling a little lonely lately."

"Even with all of your friends?" Jane asked as she parked the car in one of the vacant spots in front of Bobby's house.

Tara shrugged. "I suppose they're not the kind of friends I want."

Realization dawned. "Oh." In twenty-some years, Jane had never known Tara to be lonely, to want the comfort of a male "friend" in her life. She had always been-so caught up in life, in her art and in Jane. But of course she'd want companionship, love.

Really, who didn't?

Jane walked around the car and opened the door for her mother. Tara took her daughter's hand and they walked up the path toward the house. "It's been a long time since I put my oar in, so to speak."

"I don't think much has changed. There still are sharks out there." Jane grinned. "But every once in a while you snag a great catch."

Tara laughed. "I like this metaphor. Goes well with my Piscean nature." She squeezed Jane's hand, then said softly, "So you don't mind? I have your blessing to date?"

"Not that you need it, but of course you do. Go fishing, Mom."

"Fishing!" came a weathered, though highly masculine voice from the porch.

Jane looked up and saw Abel Garret leaning against the railing. He smiled at them both. "You two have plans with a few horses today. No skipping out for trout, understand?"

If he only knew to what they referred, Jane mused with a laugh. She turned to Tara, who looked a little flushed all of a sudden. "Mom, this is Abel Garret. Abel's the foreman here at KC Ranch."

"Among other things." Abel, aware that Tara was blind, shot down the stairs like a man half his age and took Tara's hand in his own. "Pleasure, ma'am."

Tara groaned, then laughed.

"What'd I say?" Abel asked Jane, perplexed.

Jane grimaced. "Ma'am."

"Makes me feel very old, Mr. Garret," Tara said, her face shining with humor and good health.

"Ah, I see." Abel's gaze remained on Tara, smiling at her as if she could see him. "Don't look a day over twenty-nine, but how bout this? How about I call you Tara and you can call me Abel?"

Tara grinned. "Deal…Abel."

All of a sudden, Jane felt like a third wheel. She'd heard of such a feeling, but had never experienced it. Abel and Tara were standing close, seemingly unaware of her presence, talking quietly about the ranch and Abel's job. They seemed not to even know that Jane was still there.

Jane didn't want to interrupt them, but she wanted to find Bobby. She was glad he'd had Abel call and invite her to the ranch today, glad that he'd let his wall and his pride crumble a little and admit that he wanted to see her again. Granted, she still wasn't exactly sure what was going to happen with them, but just the fact that he'd made this step gave her some hope.

Turning to Abel she asked, "Is Bobby around?"

Abel came out of his dream-like state long enough to nod, though his gaze remained on Tara. "At the paddock. Why don't you head down there?"

"Mom?" Jane said, touching her mother's arm. "Ready?"

"I got some lemonade up here on the porch," Abel put in quickly. "Tara, if you're interested…"

"Fresh-squeezed?" Tara asked.

Abel tried to look aghast. "This is the country, little lady. Is there anything else?"

Tara shook her head, then said, "And by the way, I like 'little lady.' Much better than ma'am."

They both laughed, and it was Jane's turn to shake her head. Her mother was actually flirting, full-on. Jane wasn't sure if Abel was a shark or a good catch, but she'd definitely find out the answer from his boss.

"All right," she said finally. "I'll go and find Bobby."

They both waved at her as she walked away, then Abel took Tara's hand and led her up the porch steps. Jane went around the side of the house and down the path.

The ranch was quiet, and she wondered where all the children were. Abel had told her they were understaffed today with an extra-large group of kids. Come to think of it, she mused, there weren't many cars parked in front of the house.

As she headed down the path and toward the paddock, she ran smack into Bobby. Surprise registered on his face. So did discomfiture and, if she wasn't mistaken, a desperate hunger.

"Jane."

"Hi."

He stared at her, then said a little too caustically, "What are you doing here?"

Eight

Jane was like a breath of cool air on his hot and sweaty skin. She made the sun shine frustratingly brighter and made his gut tighten with a need he knew would only keep intensifying in her company.

"Abel said you could use another pair of hands." She studied his face, a slow disappointment settling deeper and deeper into her wide green eyes. "You didn't do the inviting, did you?"

His jaw worked. "No."

She said nothing, just nodded slowly, then turned around and walked away from him.

Bobby followed her. "Jane, wait a minute."

Stumbling over a large rock, she righted herself and muttered a terse, "No."

"Where are you going?"

"To the car," she said, her chin lifted as she stalked down the path.

"Why? You're here now. Stay." He cursed under his breath. "I want you to stay."

She whirled around and eyed him critically. "Look, I don't play games. Never have. I think they're a total waste of time. You either want to see me or you don't. And after last night, I think I deserve an answer."

Frustration seeped into Bobby's pores. He spotted the barn to his right and grabbed her hand. "Come with me."

"I don't think so."

But he wasn't listening. She struggled to free her hand as he tugged her toward the barn, as he kicked open the door and as he pulled her inside. Once there, he eased her back against an empty stall door, his hands falling to either side of her shoulders as he gave her no way out and only one thing to look at.

His eyes blazed into hers. "Just because I didn't do the inviting, doesn't mean I don't want you here."

"Doesn't it?" she tossed back at him.

"Hell, Jane, I wanted you all night long. I just…"

"You just what?" she prompted brusquely, her eyes narrowed. "Because I'd really like to know why you took me home after what I thought was a really great night."

What did he say? That he was freaked out? That their conversation had traveled a road that made him wince, that he liked her, craved her, wanted nothing more than to kick his plans to the curb and jump on this idea of him and her, together…?

Jane crossed her arms over her chest. "Either answer me or let me go."

Her green eyes sparked with anger, her tall, toned body was rigid, and her mouth—that sexy, full mouth—quirked. Bobby struggled with the tension that was building inside him, and lost. He didn't think, just reacted. His mouth closed on hers, hard and demanding, as his hands left the stall door and curled around her waist and back.

At first, Jane remained still under him, her lips tight and closed, then she seemed to crumple, her lips parting, her breath quickening as she gave in to the pressure of his mouth.

Lightning fire shot up between his thighs at her response, and he tightened his hold on her. This was why he hadn't asked her to come to KC Ranch today. This was why he'd taken her home far earlier than he'd wanted to last night. She did something to him, made him forget who he was and what he had to do.

The ire inside him only fueled his desire further, and he opened his mouth, let his tongue explore the seam between her lips, so soft, so smooth, so tantalizing. She groaned with satisfaction and plunged her fingers into his hair, gripping his scalp.

Just when he thought she was going to press his face closer, she did the opposite. She pulled his head away, and raised an eyebrow at him.

"Was that an apology?" she asked, her breathing labored, her eyes liquid with the same desire that was running through his blood.

"Could be."

"Better be."

The exchange amused him, and he grinned. "Did it work? Am I forgiven?"

"I don't know," she said slowly, the pads of her thumbs caressing the tops of his cheekbones. "The punishment for being a closed-off jackass last night should be more than a little kiss."

"Little kiss?" he repeated arrogantly, his fingers gripping her back.

"You heard me." She stared at him. "No more mixed signals, Callahan."

"No." That promise was going to be the death of him. He slid his thigh between her legs and nudged at the soft V. "You want to go riding?"

A smile touched her lips. "Are we talking horses or something else?"

He gave her a wicked smile, his thigh shifting back and forth over the core of her. "First one, then the other."

"What about the work I was called here to do?" she whispered, her cheeks flushed.

"Next group is in two hours."

"Two hours?" Jane repeated, smiling. "Abel failed to mention that."

Bobby leaned in, nuzzled her neck, and reveled in the quick smack of her pulse against his mouth. "He's got a notion he needs to matchmake."

On a soft sigh, Jane managed to say, "We're way past that."

"Yes" he muttered, nipping, suckling his way back to her mouth. "We're into soul mate territory now."

Jane's breath hitched.

Bobby held her steady gaze for a moment.

What the hell had made him say something like that?

After all, he didn't believe in all that romantic, greeting-card baloney.

Teeth gritted, he meditated on an alarming query. Was it possible that his two worlds were suddenly colliding—the fact and the fantasy?

He never got the time to seek an answer. Jane had snaked her arms around his neck and was pulling his mouth down, down, down atop hers once again.

The sun beat down on Jane's back, hot and inescapable.

Today, she had her own horse. Though she'd loved sitting behind Bobby yesterday, her arms wrapped around his waist, her cheek to his back, she'd wanted to experience something new, to learn and to impress the man beside her with her fabulous equestrian skills.

And she'd only fallen off once.

Oddly, her horse had stopped short in front of a particularly large cactus. Thank goodness they'd only been walking, or no doubt she'd have ended up with more than a scratch on the hand.

"Let's give the horses a rest," Bobby said after they'd ridden for a while. "There's a lake just over that rise. We could have a swim."

She grinned. "No showers out here, I suppose?"

"City gal," Bobby needled playfully, looking entirely too sexy in his worn jeans and white T-shirt, every inch of him bronzed skin and hard muscle as he rode his gray stallion as though he'd been born atop him. "You know, if you want to be a real cowgirl, you can't expect any fancy showers on the trail."

"Who says I want to be a cowgirl?" She tossed the

words out as they rode over the rise and down to a kidney-bean-shaped lake, its water very clear and calm.

"That's right," he said, finding her gaze. "You're not sure you're going to end up in Texas, are you?"

She shook her head, sighed. "Not sure where I'm going to end up, period."

Bobby turned his gaze from her, and pointed to the lake. "You know, you can't go in there with your clothes on."

"No, I suppose not."

"Water looks great, though," he remarked, swinging his leg over the saddle and jumping down.

"I have no aversion to skinny-dipping, Mr. Callahan," Jane said as Bobby helped her down from the beautiful chestnut mare. He tethered the horses then returned to stand close in front of her.

"And I have no aversion to watching you," said Bobby in delighted, wicked tones. "Although, joining you sounds damn good, too."

"Hmm. I don't know about skinny-dipping with company," she teased. "That's a whole different matter."

His mouth curved into a sexy smile as he found the edge of her pale-blue tank top and slowly inched it upward. "There's mean fish in that lake."

"Is that so?"

He nodded, mock concern threading his tone. "Who'll protect you?"

"Good point." She raised her arms above her head and, with her heart smacking excitedly against her ribs, she allowed him to remove her tank top.

Bobby tossed the fabric onto a rock, then shifted his gaze to the top button of her jeans. "Shall I continue?"

"I think I can handle it from here," she said, unzipping her jeans, wondering when Bobby would follow suit, wondering how he would look naked under all this sunshine. "So, what's the probability of anyone seeing us?"

"Zero," Bobby told her. "No one comes out this far but me and Abel and, as you said, he's pretty occupied with your mother."

Jane forgot about her bra and panties. In fact, she forgot to breathe as she watched Bobby remove his shirt. Ridiculously, time seemed to slow, and the faint strains of an Al Green love song played in her head. Cut and bronzed, Bobby Callahan was a sight to behold. The only time she'd seen him without his clothes had been their evening in bed at the Turnbolts' where it had been dark, and she'd had to feel her way. With greedy eyes, she surveyed him—barrel-chested, with just a sprinkling of dark hair around his nipples and down to his navel. She swallowed thickly, her breasts tingling as she imagined brushing the hard tips back and forth against his chest.

Her fingers ached to grab at his stomach, so rock-hard, it looked as though he'd been slashed with a woman's fingernails. She watched his hands move lower, to his belt buckle. Off went the strip of worn leather, down went the zipper. Her throat was strained, her chest, too, as she watched him remove his jeans and the tight cotton shorts beneath. She sucked in a breath as her gaze moved up. Solid calves, powerful thighs and the thick, demanding muscle in between.

"Hey there."

She looked up, dazed, her cheeks as hot as the rest of her.

He was grinning at her. "This ain't no peep show."

"Right," was all she could manage.

"Get those skivvies off and let's go swimming."

He was at the water's edge in seconds, then dove beneath the clear blue before Jane could even register what he'd said.

Waiting until he dove under once again, Jane quickly removed her bra and panties and hurried down to the water. But she was only up to her ankles in the cool lake, when Bobby surfaced. When he saw her, her breasts moving as she walked, the dark curls between her legs, sexual awareness darkened his face.

He dove under the water again and resurfaced before her. Without a word, he eased her into his arms and held her to him, though his eyes remained fixed on hers. "I don't think I've seen you until today."

She laughed, wrapped her legs lightly around his waist. "I was thinking the same thing."

"Disappointed?" he asked with a devilish grin, as if he knew the answer.

"Get serious," she said, every inch of her electrified with the sensation of his wet skin against hers, and the center of him now hard as steel at her belly.

He pushed a strand of hair out of her eye. "You know, Kimmy and I used to swim here when we were kids. Dad taught her, was real careful with her, but she didn't want any of it."

"She sounds like she was an amazing girl."

"Yeah. Tough girl. Real loving, too."

"I wish I could've met her."

His eyes went soft, and he caressed her cheek with the pad of his thumb. "She would've liked you."

"Why do you say that?"

"Kimmy had a soft spot for funny, kind…good people, I guess."

A bashful smile tugged at Jane's mouth. The way he talked to her, about her, made her feel so cared for, and the way he touched her, gently yet possessively, made her want only to kiss him. Her arms went around his neck and she pressed herself closer to the blunt, plum-shaped tip of him. "Do you have a soft spot, Bobby?" she whispered close to his mouth, near that slash of a scar that so intrigued her.

"I'm looking at her."

His hand moved down her back, rolled over her buttocks and underneath where fine hair gave way to the slick entrance to her body. Jane arched her back, closed her eyes as she felt his fingers get closer.

"This is another one of my soft spots," Bobby whispered in her ear as he slipped one thick finger inside her.

A moan escaped Jane's throat and she pumped her hips, back and forth, taking him in and out of her body. Bobby's tongue lapped lightly at her ear, a sensation that was entirely new to Jane—a sensation that had her on the verge of orgasm in seconds.

"And this," he breathed into her ear. "This is very, very soft."

He continued to lick and nibble at her ear as he

pushed a second and third finger inside her. He was so deep, the tips of his fingers flicking back and forth against a spot so highly sensitive, Jane thought she might pass out.

She gripped his shoulder, needed the support, then felt a desperate urge to touch him as he was touching her. Down her hand raked, over his chest and belly until she found him, his erection, thick and pulsing. She wrapped her hand around him, stroked from the base to the top, circling her thumb over the smooth hood until she felt something hot and sticky-wet, so different from the lake water, drip from the tip.

"So soft, so hard," she uttered, feeling weak and ready to give in.

Her sex pulsed as he thrust his fingers inside her, smacked and teased and tormented at the spot that ached and felt electric. Despite the cool water, she was sweltering. She pumped him as he pumped her, and listened to his breath run ragged. She arched, hovered on the brink....

"Come with me," Bobby whispered against her throat as he placed the pad of his thumb on the plump ridge of nerves beneath her dark hair.

Yes. Yes.

She couldn't speak. Climax was upon her. Her muscles stiffened, inside and out, and she released an unabashed cry into the sunshine and blue sky. Bobby followed, his body convulsing in ocean-like waves, his shaft throbbing in her hand.

Passion spread like wildfire over his face, made his eyes burn blue flames as he gave in, his mouth capturing hers in such an all-consuming way, Jane would have sworn she was having her soul ripped from her body.

They lay together in a patch of sunlight, feeling lazy and comfortable and not at all ready to leave, but…

"The horses are restless," Jane said, drowsily.

Bobby rose up on an elbow and looked down at her, so bone-weakeningly sexy in nothing more than a few specks of grass. "I hate to say it—God knows I do—but it is getting late. We should head back."

"We could always come again," Jane said, then realized the double meaning in her words and laughed.

"And again and again and again." Bobby followed, chuckling.

Her gaze moved over him in a way that had his laughter turning to awareness. "All right, now," he began warily. "You better put some clothes on or I'll forget I have a bunch of kids waiting for me."

She looked horrified. "You can't do that."

"I know." He pitched her tank top at her, along with her jeans. "Hurry it up now."

They both dressed quickly and were back atop their horses riding for home when Bobby turned to her and asked, "Do you still want to help out with the kids? You don't have to. After all, Abel really tricked—"

"I want to stay, Bobby," she told him in all sincerity.

He nodded, feeling as if he'd won the lottery today. The lake had never felt so cool, the sun had never been so pleasingly warm and he'd never felt so wanted by anyone in his life. Jane was a woman without inhibitions. She didn't need rose petals or Frank Sinatra. She gave of herself, totally and freely. She took what she needed, but made certain her partner felt every ounce of her pleasure in his own.

She was rare.

And he didn't deserve to touch her.

They arrived back at the ranch in just under twenty minutes. The first thing Bobby saw was a tall blond woman in her fifties standing outside the corral fence with Abel. She was brushing down Missy, a sweet black Morgan. She looked unsure of herself with the horse, but she was laughing with Abel—as though they'd known each other for much longer than an hour or two.

Bobby hadn't met her, but he was pretty sure the woman was Jane's mother, Tara Hefner. And upon closer inspection, he saw that she had Jane's mouth and her long, lean body.

Jane was off her horse as soon as they reached the pair. "Mom, what are you doing?"

"What does it look like I'm doing?" Tara said with a laugh, looking in Jane's direction.

"But you're afraid of horses. I thought you were just going to get the kids ready with helmets and stuff."

Abel smiled at Tara and patted Missy. "Is that so, Tar? 'Fraid of horses? Well, you sure fooled me. I thought you'd been around these lugs your whole life."

Tara blushed and shook her head. "Oh, Abel."

Clearly shocked, and maybe even a little bothered by the expeditious intimacy of the pair, Jane took her mother's hand and led her over to Bobby. "Mom, I'd like you to meet someone. This is Bobby Callahan."

Like her daughter, Tara Hefner was a very beautiful,

fine-figured woman. She stuck her hand out, and said in a warm voice, "Hi, Bobby."

Bobby softened in Tara's presence, couldn't help it. She had a Southern femaleness about her, and he understood right away why Abel was acting crazy. Heck, her daughter had that sweet openness, too.

He shook her hand. "It's good to know you, Mrs. Hefner."

"I hope you don't mind another assistant?"

"Not at all. In fact, my daddy used to say, 'It don't take a genius to spot a ready angel in a flock of weary sheep.'"

That made her smile, and she leaned close to him, whispering, "Your father sounds like a good man."

"I like to think so," Bobby said tightly, not missing the quizzical look Jane gave him.

Little more was said as the children arrived. Bobby put Jane to work immediately, assisting with the preparations and mounting. From time to time, he'd glance her way, his gut tightening with pride as he watched her, so gentle as she encouraged a young girl from her wheelchair and onto the back of Dandy, an old white mare. She was comfortable here already, comfortable with him, his life and his body. Heat surged into his blood as a flash of memory from this afternoon entered his mind.

He forced his gaze away, onto Abel and Tara, who were working as a team. While Abel led two horses around the paddock, Tara held onto the top of the stirrup, talking to the young boy in the saddle.

It was a sight for sad eyes.

This place hadn't seen the likes of Tara and Jane for a long time and everything here, kids, horses and staff alike seemed to blossom under their care.

Bobby lifted Kitty Johnson onto the back of an old quarter horse, his gut twisting painfully as he realized that the promise he'd made to his father would soon rip this wonderful, short-lived reality from his sights for good.

Nine

It was close to sundown when a weary Tara and a beaming Jane returned to the house of Al-Nayhal. The lush and highly polished surroundings felt just a little chilly after the warm modesty of KC Ranch. Especially when Sakir Al-Nayhal, dressed in a flowing white kaftan, met them at the front door, his face set with grim determination.

"Good evening, sister, Tara." He nodded at each of them, his gaze so stern it caused Jane's cheerful mood to fade slightly.

It was no mystery what was about to happen. Under the priceless chandelier, another confrontation between her and her brother over Jane's choice of man was about to take place. But after the wonderful time she'd had today, she was more than armed to fight him.

"Good evening, Sakir," Tara said quickly, obviously sensing the tension in the air. "Is Rita with us?"

"No, she is with the baby. Daya is having trouble sleeping."

"Ah," Tara said sagely, turning toward Jane. "I remember many a night walking the hallway with you in my arms."

"Just didn't want to sleep," Jane explained to Sakir. "I was always a problem child."

"That's not true," Tara defended passionately.

Jane laughed. "But I grew out of it."

"I am not so sure," Sakir said softly, then when he had captured Jane's attention, continued, "You worked at KC Ranch this afternoon, did you not?"

"Yes."

A heavy sigh was followed by a glance in Tara's direction. "Please talk some sense into your daughter, Tara."

Tara smiled patiently. "It's not that simple, Sakir."

"It must be."

"Just wait until your Daya grows up. You'll see that once they are adults, you have little influence over their decisions."

Sakir lifted his chin and stated proudly, "It will not be so with my daughter."

Tara's smile widened. "Well, I think I'm going to head upstairs. It's been a long day."

"Wait," Jane said, reaching for her mother's hand. "I'll take you up."

"That is not necessary." Sakir clapped his hands three times and Marian appeared in the doorway. "Please take Ms. Hefner to her room."

Marian inclined her head, then went to Tara's side, rested her hand on the older woman's arm. "Ms. Hefner?"

"Goodnight," Tara said to the both of them with a touch of hesitancy in her voice. "Be kind to each other."

Knowing it was important to reassure her mother that everything was going to be all right, Jane used a phrase from her childhood. "Sleep tight, Mom."

Tara granted her a nod and a loving smile before following the housekeeper up the stairs.

When she was gone, Sakir motioned for Jane to follow him into the living room, where a healthy blaze crackled and snapped in the fireplace. Jane sat beside him on a long, gray chenille sofa and waited for him to say whatever it was that he needed to say.

It didn't take long.

"You are falling for him, yes?"

Eyebrows knit together, Jane laughed. "Where did you hear that expression?"

"My wife has said this. About you and...Callahan."

"Has she?"

"She thinks you are in love." He leaned back, crossed his arms over his chest. "I cannot allow this, Jane. I only accepted your dates with Bobby Callahan because I thought that would be all of it. Just a few casual outings. After all, the man has never taken any woman seriously since I have known him."

Alert now, Jane straightened in her seat. "How would you know that?"

With a dismissive flip of the hand, Sakir uttered, "I have ways of finding out information."

The heat from the fire seemed to intensify as Jane absorbed this news. If all Bobby Callahan had been able to manage until now was a date or two, then she was in luck. Aside from the dates they'd shared, Bobby had actually sought her out—at the mall with Rita—and had shared his personal history with her. Those were not the acts of a casual affair.

"Jane?"

She looked into her brother's dark eyes with their wary expression, and grinned like a teenager. "So, he had no serious girlfriends in the past, huh?"

Realizing that the information he'd given her as a warning had only managed to spur her on, Sakir shot her a penetrating stare. "You do not take this matter seriously."

"Oh, believe me, Sakir, I take this very seriously."

Clearly he didn't believe her, because a moment later he was shaking his head and muttering foolish threats. "I am afraid I will have to forbid you from seeing him again."

Unable to stop herself, Jane burst out laughing. "Oh, c'mon, Sakir."

"I am in earnest."

"You're talking like it's the nineteenth century and you're my guardian."

"As your brother I have the right to make decisions, even demands."

Suddenly Jane's laughter died, and so did her smile. She looked at him. Really looked. He wasn't kidding. And this wasn't a quirky brother-sister squabble over what was best for Jane. This was Sheikh Al-Nayhal making an edict.

Her gaze fixed to his, Jane spoke gravely to her brother. "Understand something, please. You have no rights over me. I love you, Sakir, but I'm an adult."

As if he hadn't heard her, Sakir continued, "While you are under my roof—"

"Please don't go there."

"Jane."

"I'm serious, Sakir. That's a dangerous road to take."

"So is the one you are traveling on," he snapped. "Our father would not allow this—"

"I have no father," she interrupted, her tone dotted with a sourness she never knew she possessed. But the truth of the matter was she would never consider the wishes of a parent who had not been in her life—or a brother who hardly knew her, yet believed he knew what was best for her.

"You may not have known the great sultan," Sakir said tightly. "But he would not have allowed such a thing to continue, and I'm afraid I cannot allow it, either."

They stared at each other, stubborn green eyes to dictatorial ones. Finally, Jane stood and nodded. "I'll leave first thing in the morning."

A dark-red stain moved over Sakir's face. "I will not allow that, either."

She said nothing, couldn't say anything with the lump of misery in her throat. Her new family was causing her tremendous pain, forcing her to look at difficult choices.

But the choice to walk away from Sakir, in that moment, was the easiest one she knew she'd ever make.

"We're a couple of sorry saps."

"How do you figure that?" Bobby asked. He and Abel sat on the porch steps, stars flickering in the sky above, beers in hand, just as they'd done almost every night since the older man had come to work at KC Ranch.

Gloom curled through Abel's voice. "Another night with no women."

"Speak for yourself. I was out last night," Bobby reminded him.

"And where's that pretty little filly tonight?"

"Back at Al-Nayhal's."

Hearing the irritation in Bobby's voice, Abel rolled his lips under his teeth. "You know, that Tara's a nice-looking woman."

"You think so, do you?"

"I do. Nicest-looking woman I've seen since…" Abel's voice drifted off and he looked slightly pained at the near mention of his ex-wife, and understandably so. He'd loved her something awful.

"Maybe you should do something about it," Bobby suggested, thinking that the man deserved some home and hearth after what he'd been through.

"Maybe."

"What's the problem?" Bobby asked, his tone threaded with a challenge. "You scared to go under the knife again?"

Abel tipped his beer bottle back and took a swig. "Too old to get my guts ripped out."

"Yeah, I can see that."

Catching the grin on Bobby's face, Abel chuckled. "But then again, I don't want to end up like you, either."

Shifting on the creaky wooden step, Bobby shot Abel a glare of reproach. "What the hell does that mean?"

"One woman to the next. You hardly get to know 'em before you say adios."

Bobby gave a defensive shrug. "Haven't found the right girl, that's all. Not that it's any of your business."

As usual, Abel ignored the last comment. "Jane looks pretty right to me."

To Bobby, too.

Damn her.

Visions of tangled legs, wet fingers and a strange familiarity that went far past the physical, shot into his brain.

Damn her.

There was nothing wrong with good old-fashioned sex. Nothing wrong with a day of fun out on the lake. Nothing, except the ties that bind you, force you closer, worm their way inside your brain and stop you from thinking about anything else.

That's what was happening with Jane. He couldn't think about anything or anyone else. He wanted more—more of her hands on him, more of the laughter in her eyes, more of that heart that practically sang with compassion and truth.

On a trashy curse, he shoved his empty beer can into Abel's hand and mumbled, "I'll see you later."

As he stalked down the path to the driveway, Abel called after him, "Where you going?"

"Need to clear my head," Bobby shot back over his shoulder.

"If it were only that easy," Bobby heard the man say with a dry chuckle as he headed for his truck.

The weight of him pressing down on her body nearly had her breathless.

Wet, wonderful kisses blanketed Jane's mouth as she

wrapped her legs around his waist and thrust her hips up. Bobby entered her slowly, inch by glorious inch, and she reveled in the sweet invasion.

Then, in a red flash, they were fully clothed and Bobby was ripped from her by Sakir. In one disjointed movement, Sakir plowed his fist into Bobby's gut. A low groan erupted from Bobby's throat, and he went at Sakir like a defensive lineman. Jane watched helplessly as the two men fought without fear and without tiring for what seemed like an eternity.

Suddenly she *was Bobby, and she was the one fighting her brother with all the strength of a man. She felt his bone-crushing blows to her jaw and ribs. She felt the sadness, horror and adrenaline that kept her from running, kept her fighting even when her body cried in pain, even as tears washed her cheeks....*

"Hey, hey there, darlin'."

Jane's eyes flew open; she was instantly relieved of her nightmare. She was in her room, the scents of fresh bed linen and night air curling through her senses.

But there was something else.

Someone else.

Her heart smacked against her ribs and she sat up, stared into the blue gaze of the very man she had been dreaming about. "Ohmigod, Bobby."

"Shhh..." he said, placing a finger to her lips, looking around at the door and the window.

Jane glanced at the clock. Eleven forty-five. Then back at him. "How did you get into my room?"

"Through the window."

Not sure she'd heard him correctly, she tilted her

head to see past him to the open window. "I'm on the second floor, and there's a guard and dogs."

"That's right." His gaze, so dark and intense, slipped to her mouth. He reached out, traced the edge of her jaw with his fingertip. "That's how badly I needed to see you?"

Reality dawned. He was really here, in her room, on her bed. "Is something wrong or—"

His finger moved up, flicked gently over her lower lip. "Nothing's wrong, darlin'. I just needed to give you something."

"What is it?"

"This." With gentle hands, he eased her back to the mattress once again. His eyes filled with wicked intent, he hovered above her, his thigh nestled between her legs.

"And this," he uttered, his mouth greedily descending on hers.

Ten

All that Jane wanted was to have him inside her.

Ever since that night—that party at the Turnbolts'—she'd wondered if those delicious quakes and shivers she'd experienced lying beneath Bobby, the way her blood had roared in her brain like a starved animal, had been real, or just a product of her overly romantic thought processes.

Jane gazed down and sucked air between her teeth, her skin hot and electric at the sight before her. Bobby lay cradled between her legs, blazing a trail of kisses from her knee to her trembling inner thigh.

Her womb ached at the sight—there was no other way to describe the feeling, but it was one she'd never experienced before. Strong and pulsing, running straight from brain to blood.

She realized that the Turnbolts' party had been just a prequel to this night. A fusion of not just two bodies, but two souls, two minds and, if she got her way, two hearts.

"You're so sweet, Jane," whispered Bobby against the hot skin of her thigh as he nuzzled his way, nipping and suckling, to the center of her.

Perhaps it was a purely sexual urge, perhaps she was desperate to connect with him, but Jane rose up on her elbows to watch him. With gentle hands he splayed her thighs and dipped his head.

Electric heat shot through her as tongue met the hard band of her sex. The groans and breathy sounds didn't feel as though they were coming from her, but the strain of her throat proved otherwise. Her gaze moved over Bobby. His hands on her hips, the pads of his fingers digging deliciously into the flesh of her buttocks, his dark head buried between her thighs.

His tongue was creating a trail of fire as he raked up and down the hooded tangle of nerves. His movements were ruthless and hungry, and Jane felt her hips lift, felt them pump against his mouth, move and jerk out of instinct alone.

She let her head fall back, her hand fisting his hair, slamming him harder against her.

Bobby had never had a woman take what she wanted in such a bold, open way. As Jane pumped and writhed against his mouth, she left no doubt of her need for him, and he adored her for it.

"Please," she breathed.

"How do you want this, darlin'?" said Bobby, his

groin tight, his cock straining against the zipper of his jeans as the salty tang of her invaded his nostrils. "My mouth or my—"

"I want *you*. Inside me."

That's what Bobby wanted, too. Maybe he was a fool for caring so much, for needing this woman the way he did. But he couldn't help himself. As he slipped on a condom, he realized how much he wanted to remember tonight, the way he'd loved her, the way he'd given himself to her as he knew he could never do out of bed.

But all his thoughts and sorry hopes vanished as Jane wriggled beneath him, her hips arching with a need that hadn't yet been fulfilled. Bobby's gaze slipped to the entrance to her body, glistening wet and pink. Fear mingled with the rock-hard need possessing every muscle in his body. Joining with her, pushing into the tight, scalding glove of her body, meant more to him than he'd ever thought possible.

For one brief moment, he thought about burying his head once again between her beautiful thighs, sending her to the heavens with his tongue and fingers. But her eyes were on him, burning with a raging fire that ran through his blood, as well.

She spread her legs wide and reached for him. "Please, Bobby."

"Yes. Yes, sweetheart." With one sure thrust, he pushed through the tight passageway and found heaven.

"Bobby," she uttered, her muscles closing around him in a gentle fist.

Bobby's mind went numb, blood pounded in his ears. All thoughts of revenge and guilt and lust and hope seeped out of his mind and left him with nothing but a soothing euphoria.

His mouth tucked into her neck, his erection poised deep inside her body, he whispered, "Tell me you're not going to leave this time."

"No. I'm not going anywhere," she said, clinging to him, pumping her hips slowly, urging him to move.

And he could deny himself no longer. He rose up and slammed back down. Over and over, he thrust inside her. Damp flesh slapping against damp flesh. The sound, mingled with Jane's cries, drove him mad.

Bobby knew they could be heard, and muffled the sounds of her pleasure with his mouth. A red haze blanketed the room, coated his mind. And he shook, hard and long. Felt Jane shudder, the muscles around him quaked as she climaxed. Then he was coming, intense and hot, his own shout of pleasure softened by her deep kiss.

Minutes rolled by, maybe longer, Bobby wasn't certain. He felt drained, and as though he never wanted to move again. He couldn't recall ever feeling so satisfied, so alive. And the feeling scared the hell out of him.

"Bobby?"

His gaze found hers, sleepy and lush. "Yes, darlin'?"

She cupped his cheek in her palm. "There's something I've got to ask you."

"All right."

Her smile was slow and not a little bit sensual. "Were you infiltrating the enemy's fortress tonight?"

He matched her smile, though his gut twisted with a twinge of guilt. "It's no secret that I'm not welcome here. And yes, I feel some satisfaction that I got up here, to you, without being detected. But believe me when I say that my reason for climbing that tree was all about seeing you, darlin'."

"You missed me?"

"Damn right."

"Good." She kissed him, slow and sexy, then whispered, "But maybe you should go now."

Rolling to his back on the bed, Bobby chuckled. "Not the thing a man wants to hear right after making love."

The playfulness in her eyes vanished, and her shoulders fell. "I know, but I can't handle another confrontation tonight."

"What do you mean, another?"

She sighed. "Sakir and I got into a fight earlier."

"About me?"

She gave him a grim smile. "No, about me. He wants to impose his brotherly wisdom on me."

Irritation slammed into him as her discord became his. "He wants you to stay away from the cowboy on his land."

"*Wants* is the relaxed version," said Jane. "He actually demanded that I never see you again, as if I was twelve."

"Maybe to him you are," said Bobby, suddenly feeling as though he'd made a mistake in coming here tonight. He hated that he'd caused her pain, caused a rift between her and her brother. He was actually beginning to despise himself more than he did Sakir.

"So, what did you tell him?" said Bobby, self-recrimination making his tone sharper than he wanted. "Because this won't be our last meeting."

Her eyebrows rose at the obvious possessiveness in his tone, but she didn't refute it. "I told him I was an adult, and that I'll make my own decisions, choices and mistakes."

Mistakes. The word cut through Bobby like a chainsaw.

With a shrug, Jane said, "I just need some space from him, that's all."

Bobby glanced around. "Well, this house is big enough for it."

"I don't think so. I told him I was leaving."

Bobby was so shocked he actually sat up. "What?" he said angrily. "Where are you going?"

"Probably to a hotel for a few days."

Relief that she wasn't leaving town altogether spread through him like warm honey, and he relaxed momentarily. But only momentarily because a realization assaulted him. He wasn't angry over the thought that her absence meant his plan failing. No, he was angry at the thought of days and nights without her.

He was in the deep end, swimming with sharks.

Big trouble.

"I have the baby's party on Saturday to plan," Jane was saying. "So, I have to stay close."

"You're still going to do that party?"

"Of course I am," she said strongly. "Daya is my niece. Granted, this whole thing with Sakir puts a damper on matters, but I've never been one to walk away from a commitment."

No, he'd just bet she hadn't.

"You're not going to any hotel, Jane." The words and

their meaning were out of his mouth before he could take them back.

She sighed and moved away from him to the edge of the bed. "Don't you start, too."

"I'm not bossing, Jane, I'm asking you to stay with me."

The smile she granted him could have lit a dark, Texas sky. "Bobby, that's sweet of you, but—"

"The hell with sweet," he barked good-naturedly, shoving off the bed and coming to his feet. "It's purely selfish. I may've made it sound like it was easy before, but if I have to climb up that trellis one more time I might just end up losing my best bits."

As she watched him yank on his jeans, she laughed. "And we can't have that."

"No, indeed."

She inhaled deeply, shrugged. "I don't know. My mom's got to be with—"

"You and Tara can stay in Abel's house," Bobby told her quickly. "It's private, but close enough to the main house for whatever you might need."

"Bobby, I don't know…"

"Yes, you do." He grinned, tucking in his flannel shirt. "It's a damn good plan and you know it."

Bobby watched as ten different emotions crossed her face while she weighed the pros and cons of such an offer. Then finally, she smiled. "Okay."

"Good. I'll be by for you around seven."

"No. We'll come to you."

Understanding her need for independence right now, Bobby nodded, then leaned over and gave her a kiss before heading out the window and down the trellis. A grin tugged at his mouth. He couldn't have asked for anything more. Jane close by, at his home and on his land, and the sweet knowledge that they were both making Sakir Al-Nayhal pay for his commands and arrogance.

For Jane, leaving her brother's house had been an incredibly difficult move. Rita had been angry with her husband for his foolishness and had on several occasions that morning tried to make him see reason and retract his demands on Jane. But he was resolute. He believed Bobby was out to hurt Jane, and Sakir had made it clear that he wouldn't stand by and watch it happen.

For just a brief moment, Sakir's resolve had caused Jane to wonder about the man she was falling in love with, had caused her heart to flip-flop with fear. But she'd forced herself to look at the reality of the past few weeks, and had come to the conclusion that her fear was just her insecurity talking.

As she'd walked Jane to the rental car, Rita had made her promise that this move would be temporary. While Jane made her sister-in-law see that it was Sakir's decision and fence to mend, Jane assured Rita that she would continue to plan little Daya's party from Bobby's place.

Tara stayed relatively silent on the drive, though she kept her hand over Jane's for most of the way in reassurance and support. After all, when it came down to it, they had been family forever, and nothing would divide them.

Pulling into KC Ranch felt good, felt right. Jane had thought she might feel beholden to Bobby, but she didn't. She was excited to see him and to be on the ranch where so much good was happening—where she felt of use to the world.

Bobby and Abel met them when they came to a dusty halt in front of the house, and helped them both out of the car.

"Welcome," Bobby said, taking Jane's hand and giving her a kiss on the cheek. "Had breakfast yet?"

"No," said Jane, her heart warming at the endearing greeting. "I'm not all that hungry, though."

Abel took Tara's hand as well and gave her a grin. "How 'bout I take you up to the house for some coffee and eggs?"

Tara glanced in Jane's direction, a wistful expression on her face. Jane recognized it at once. Whenever Tara had been away from her beloved pottery for too long, she wore that expression. "I should help Jane get unpacked."

"No, Mom," Jane assured her. "You go."

"Don't you worry, Tara," said Bobby magnanimously, heading for the trunk of the car. "I'll give her a hand."

"All right." Tara walked up the front steps with Abel, looking very pleased.

"Looks like my mother's got one heck of a crush," said Jane as she followed Bobby around the side of the house.

Carrying all three suitcases as though they were nothing more than three matchboxes, Bobby chuckled. "She's not the only one."

"Abel's got it bad?"

"Like a slap in the neck, darlin'."

They were still laughing when Bobby stopped in front of a sweet little cottage. Painted white with dark-green trim, the place was lovely. Big enough for two with lots of flowers and plants and trees, even a small vegetable garden along the side that was boasting two rows of ruby-red tomatoes.

They walked up the porch steps and Jane eyed a white porch swing. "Abel lives here?" she asked, surprise evident in her voice.

"I know. Ruddy old bachelor lives like a peacock."

"It's so neat and clean."

"His former wife's influence. Never been able to shed that thick skin." Bobby set the bags down on stripped hardwood floor. "We gave it a good cleaning, put fresh linens and towels out."

"Thank you." Feeling suddenly weary, Jane sat on the couch and rubbed her eyes.

Bobby sat beside her. "Everything'll be okay, Jane."

"You think so?"

He didn't answer her.

"A few months ago, my life ran a perfectly straight track, and now it's a damn mess. Found out about my real father, about this whole royalty thing…Emand… my brothers." Through an open window, the faint scent of hay and earth wafted in on a breeze. Jane looked up at Bobby, her head heavy, her heart, too. "I feel lost. I thought if I came to Texas—if I left Emand and that life for a while—I'd gain some perspective, be able to see that clear path again. Maybe settle into a life."

"You will," Bobby assured her, though his eyes were slow to echo that statement. "It'll come. You have to give it time. You can't expect things to jump into place minutes after they're tossed around."

A grin tugged at her mouth. "Another one of your dad's sayings?"

"Nope. That one's all me."

Her gaze ran over him, from knocked-around boots to weathered jeans and white T-shirt. He looked like the best thing she'd ever seen, and she hoped to God her brother was wrong. "Thanks, Bobby."

"For what?" he asked.

"Being a friend."

Something dark and undefined moved over his eyes and he looked away. The look unnerved her to her very bones. "Well, maybe I should unpack."

"Right." He stood quickly. "I have a few chores to finish. You'll be all right here?"

"Sure."

After he left, Jane unpacked, refusing to think about what could be. Before she went to work on her own future, she had one important task to complete.

With a steaming cup of tea in her hand, she sat at a little desk beside the open bay window and jumped into the party plans for the daughter of the man she wasn't speaking to—but the man she had come to love as a brother.

Eleven

Bobby had never had a girl in his bed before.

Sounded crazy for a man his age, but he'd always made it a practice to keep women away from his home. It had started out as a protection for his sister, but had continued as a protection for himself. And until Jane Hefner had come into his life, he'd succeeded with that practice. Hell, until Jane, he'd climbed in and out of women's beds, between their starched sheets and beside their fancy pillows.

Didn't want that anymore. Didn't want other women, and didn't want to keep his bed cold.

"So what do you think?"

Lying on the mattress, head on a pillow, Bobby gazed at the woman who had stolen his heart. She sat, legs crossed, sheet tangled, on his bed, holding a pen and a pad of paper. Bobby hated the paper. It was one of those big, yellow legal pads that blocked his view of her pale breasts and pink nipples.

He sighed, the heaviness of a day spent in lovemaking still clinging to his body. As Abel had taken Tara back to the cottage to get her settled and pack a picnic lunch, Jane had come to the main house to work on her menu for the party. But she'd only got as far as the wine and beer list before Bobby had asked her to his bed.

"Read it over again," he said, craning his neck to see over the yellow legal pad.

Jane's pen moved down the paper as she spoke. "Tender smoked brisket, cheese enchiladas, mesquite-grilled chicken, beef flautas with a red-pepper cream sauce. Beans and rice, of course, and Tara's cloverleaf rolls."

"Don't forget about the salads. Got to have a fancy coleslaw and potato salad. Those uppity types love potato salad, but they won't admit it." He took one of her soft feet in his hand and rubbed the instep. "They're so tight in the hind-parts they won't put it on their plate unless it's gourmet—like with red or purple potatoes or some such nonsense."

"Got it. Nonsense potatoes." She laughed as she wrote.

"What about desserts?"

"We're having hot peach cobbler, vanilla buttermilk pie and chocolate fudge pecan pie."

"Oh, darlin', my mouth's watering." Abandoning her foot, he reached for the yellow legal pad and pulled it down an inch or two so he could see her face, and the supple rise of her breasts. "Or maybe that's just because I'm looking at you."

She grinned. "You know your flattery will get you everywhere?"

"I'm counting on it."

Hard as stone, Bobby flipped back the sheet and grinned. Jane laughed and held her notebook up as a shield. "I still have three staff members to hire." She pointed at the ancient clock on the bedside table. "And I have to meet them in one hour."

Bobby seized her ankles and pulled her to him. "Plenty of time."

The notebook slipped from Jane's hand and landed with a dull thud on the rug as Bobby splayed her thighs, and with a wicked grin, lowered his head.

Luck was with her.

Out of the five people Jane had interviewed, she'd found three new fabulous staff members to hire. One young man who worked for his mother's restaurant, but wanted some experience elsewhere was not only going to cook, but also was actually going to act as Jane's buyer since he knew the best butchers, farmers and wholesale suppliers in town.

Things were falling into place, and Daya was going to have a wonderful party, despite all the family craziness surrounding the festivities.

"Jane?"

With a start, Jane turned. Walking up Delano Street, baby Daya in tow, was Rita. Dressed in a pale-pink track suit, the woman smiled warmly and gave Jane a big hug when they met.

Her lips tucked under her teeth contemplatively, Rita asked, "Everything okay?"

"Fine. Great, in fact." For the next several minutes, Jane filled Rita in on the new staff and the menu she'd concocted that morning in Bobby's bed. "We'll be ready to go on Saturday. I'll probably need to come over on Friday to set up."

Rita cocked her head to the side. "You're welcome anytime, you know that."

As people milled up and down the street, gazing in shop windows, laughing or scolding their children, Jane looked directly at her sister-in-law with a sad smile. "How's my brother?"

"Doesn't show his feelings much, but I can tell that he's very upset."

"I'm sure."

"He won't budge."

"He's stubborn."

Rita gave a melancholy laugh and nodded. "Yes. Please don't hate him, Jane."

"Oh, God." Shaking her head, Jane tried to explain what was so heavy on her heart. "I don't hate him. I'm not even mad at him. I just won't be dictated to. Even if this relationship with Bobby turns out exactly the way Sakir believes it will, it'll be my doing, my choice."

A proud gleam twinkled in Rita's blue eyes. "He had to get used to one strong woman in his life, and he'll do it again." She smiled at her baby. "And again, no doubt."

Jane laughed. "No doubt."

"So, how are things with Bobby?" asked Rita gingerly, her eyes twinkling once again.

Jane knew she was beaming, but she didn't care. "Wonderful."

Rita smiled. "I'm happy for you."

"Thanks." Little Daya started to fuss and the three of them walked down the street toward Market Place. The question that weighed heavily on Jane's heart finally inched its way to her lips. "Do you think it's possible to heal this rift between Sakir and Bobby?"

With a shrug, Rita said, "I don't know. Over time, maybe."

"I hope so."

A full minute passed as they crossed the street. Once at the other side, Rita paused and gave Jane a knowing smile. "So, when did you realize you were in love with him?"

Jane actually pretended to look confused for a moment, which made Rita break out into a fit of laughter. "Oh, c'mon, sis."

Tucking her arm through Rita's, Jane sighed as they walked up Grand Avenue. "Well, I guess it was the night he sneaked into your house and into my bed."

When Abel Garret had something serious on his mind, he stood stock-still, his legs splayed, his arms crossed over his chest and his eyes fixed into two narrow slits. It was a look Bobby normally paid attention to, maybe even questioned if he had the time. But today, he had a feeling Abel's mood wasn't related to troubles with KC Ranch.

"Something to say?" asked Bobby in a dry voice.

A sound close to a grunt echoed from Abel's throat. "What's going on between you two?

With a glare, Bobby pointed to himself, then the animal beside him. "Trainer, horse."

Abel scowled. "I'm talking about you and Jane."

"Right. That makes more sense."

"Callahan, you answer me."

Bobby gave the mare beside him a pat and faced his foreman. The man wore his troubled fatherly expression—the one that made Bobby experience equal parts of frustration and fondness. "I like the girl, okay?"

"I think it's far more than that, and so does her mama."

Bobby pulled off his Stetson. He felt damn hot for a relatively cool fall day. "Hasn't Jane made it clear? She doesn't want anyone interfering in this…this…whatever we got going here—and neither do I."

"Tough," said Abel brusquely.

Bobby cursed and walked away from him, toward the corral gate.

Abel followed him. "Family's always involved. May not like it, but there it is."

Swatting at an irritating pair of flies, Bobby whirled on Abel. "I don't have any family."

Abel looked as if he'd been punched, and the sight made Bobby's insides kick. He had this angry streak in him, born out of a promise he'd made to a man whose vow for vengeance wasn't altogether sure he believed in anymore, and fed by a vile bag of revenge he was about to dump on the woman who had made his life livable again.

"Listen, Abel—" he began, but the older man was having none of it.

Through gritted teeth, Abel said, "Say whatever you

want to me, but I'm serious about this girl. She's in love with you, Bobby. Sure as a shot."

Bobby's jaw tightened. He didn't want to hear it, yet he already knew that what Abel said was true.

"Just take care," Abel added with a shrug, opening the gate.

Noncommittally, Bobby nodded. "Yeah."

"I think you'd be feeling something strong for her, too, but you'll stamp that out, won't you?"

"None of your business." Abel didn't know about the vow Bobby had made to his father, but he was sure acting like he knew something.

"Fine. Fine." The older man waved him off and went down the path toward the house.

"Hey." Bobby called after him. "Where you going?"

Abel stopped, glanced over his shoulder. "Tara and I are camping out by the lake tonight. She wants to lie on her back and see the stars."

"See the stars…"

Abel smiled a little sadly. "Through me. You know, that woman may be blind, but she sees a helluva lot more than the rest of us."

Tipping his Stetson, Abel turned and headed toward the house. Leaning against the fence, Bobby reached into his pocket, took out the watch his father had given him, the one with the old man's picture inside. Bobby stared into the rugged face and felt as though the weight of his stallion leaned heavily on his back. Felt a powerful struggle deep within his heart.

What was he doing? His life, once simple and uncomplicated, had turned into a web of lies and lust and, more than possibly, love. He didn't want to look at that last part, didn't want to admit that he was going to bring down the woman he needed above all others for a man who no longer walked the earth.

But the promise—that goddamn vow—couldn't be laid to rest without acting on it.

The sound of tires on gravel had him looking up. Someone was coming up the drive. He headed in that direction, arriving just in time to see a long, black car come to an easy, money-soft stop in front of the ranch house.

At first, Bobby thought it was Sakir, and he was glad. He was ready for a war of words, maybe a few punches. He felt wired as hell.

But the man who stepped out of the Mercedes wasn't Sakir, though he sure had the look of him.

"Bobby Callahan?"

Bobby nodded. "That's right."

"I am Zayad Al-Nayhal. I wish to see my sister."

Twelve

The first thing Jane saw when she got back to KC Ranch that afternoon was Bobby, sweaty and serious out in the ring, training a particularly lovely jet-black stallion.

The second was Zayad Al-Nayhal.

Her eldest brother, the reigning Sultan of Emand, stood regally beside the steel fence in a stark-white kaftan, his chin hard, and his dark gaze intent on the animal and rider before him.

Jane's heart gave a nervous lurch, which irritated the heck out of her. She hated feeling anxious. But even though her best friend, Mariah, had softened Zayad a little, he was still an intimidating presence. Jane knew that if Zayad had come to Bobby's ranch to try to force the royal Al-Nayhal will on her, she was going to need every ounce of strength she possessed to stand up to him.

She watched him watch Bobby, an air of superiority affixed to his handsome countenance—or was it interest? She couldn't tell. But the former would no doubt be the surest guess. Zayad could not help his attitude. After all, he'd grown up in a palace with an armload of servants to do his every bidding.

What was he doing here? Jane wondered, biting her lip thoughtfully. He wasn't supposed to have arrived in Texas until Friday. Sakir must have called him, told him what had happened and asked him to come and take control of their little sister.

With a forced smile that slowly morphed into a real one, she walked up to her brother and laid a hand on his shoulder. "Well, what do we have here?"

Rarely startled, Zayad turned easily. "Hello, Jane," he said, his dark eyes intent, his tone warm. "Mr. Callahan was kind enough to allow me to watch his training session, and show me a few of his stallions. This one is a particularly beautiful beast."

He wrapped her in his arms and gave her a kiss on the cheek. "My brother has told me what transpired between you."

So, Sakir *had* called him. Not much of a shock there. "I'm sorry I wasn't at the house to greet you, but my mother and I—"

"Yes, I know," interrupted Zayad before releasing a weighty breath. "Sakir is acting the fool."

Just as Jane was about to agree, Bobby took that particular moment to ride up. He slipped from the stallion's back and joined them. "Who's a fool?"

"I was saying this about our brother," Zayad told

Bobby, his chin lifted as though he was the only human being alive who was allowed to say so.

Leaning against the fence, Jane looked at the ground. "He's no fool. He's just being protective—in his own irritating way, of course."

"Does he have reason to be protective?"

Jane's head came up. Zayad was staring at her, then he turned to look at Bobby, one dark eyebrow raised.

Bobby's mouth thinned with anger. "Your sister is more than capable of handling whatever's thrown her way."

Zayad nodded slowly. "Yes, I believe she is. She is Al-Nayhal, after all."

"Yes, she is," Bobby agreed.

A heavy weight sat on Jane's shoulders, on her heart and soul, as well. Bobby had offered neither a yes nor a no to Zayad's question about her needing to be protected. It was possible that Bobby thought the query insulting or maybe he was just too angry at the Al-Nayhals to give any of them a sign of his sincere feelings regarding their sister—Jane didn't know. But that quick, jabbing fear she seemed to experience every time she thought about Sakir's warning and Bobby's feelings reared its unwelcome head once again.

"Mariah is downtown at a restaurant called the Willow Tree." Zayad's words broke through Jane's uneasy fog. "Will you join us for a late lunch? Tara as well, if she is free."

"My mother's with a friend right now," Jane explained, thinking of Tara around the small kitchen table smiling as Abel read her another chapter of *Don Quixote*. "And there isn't much that'll tear her away from him."

Zayad gave a nod of understanding, then turned to look at Bobby. "Mr. Callahan, would you care to join us?"

"I don't think so," Bobby said, his face stoic.

"Yes, that would be wonderful," Jane said, true excitement in her tone. She turned to Bobby. "C'mon, Bobby. Mariah's my very best friend in the world. She's beautiful and pregnant and funny and a great lawyer." A wide grin split her features. "And if you're real lucky, maybe she'll tell you how she and Zayad met. He moved in next door to us in California and pretended to be just an average Joe. It's a very funny story."

With a quick roll of the eyes, Zayad explained, "Not one of my finer moments. But I received a most precious gift. My wife and a mother for my son, Redet, and our baby to come."

"So deception brought you good fortune," Bobby said, his voice threaded with a lighthearted antagonism that made Jane's stomach churn.

Zayad's face turned to stone. "Pardon me?"

Around them a breeze blew. It was neither cool nor hot, and was scented with aging hay. "Just remarking that deceit for profit seems to run in your family, that's all."

"Bobby!" Jane said sharply, shocked at his rudeness. But she was allowed nothing else as Zayad turned on the cowboy.

"You do not insult the family of Al-Nayhal," Zayad warned.

With a cold frown, Bobby nodded. "Whenever I can."

As Jane tried to think of what to say next, her belly as tight as a trap, the two men stared at each other. Both exceptionally tall, one all lean muscle, the other brawny and steeped in a bitterness he refused to climb out of.

"Bobby," Jane began hesitantly, not exactly sure what to say or do to diffuse the situation. She hardly thought a good punch in the stomach would be appropriate, but she was so frustrated at his attitude, she wished she could.

But Bobby didn't stay long enough for a word or a jab. "I have work to do," he uttered, then turned away, led the stallion toward the other end of the ring, tossing a tart, "Enjoy your lunch," over his shoulder.

Jane didn't want to look at her brother. She knew what was coming, what he was about to say, and she didn't blame him. When Zayad touched her shoulder, she found his gaze. "Jane, I do not wish to say this, but I think Sakir may be right."

She shook her head. "No. You don't understand. Bobby's had a hard time of it, Zayad. He's lost his land, his father, his sister. He's lashing out at the family he thinks is responsible for his destruction."

"Yes, I agree. And you, my girl, will no doubt get caught in the crossfire."

"I don't believe that," said Jane, not thoroughly convinced. "But even if I do, it's my choice to make."

Zayad nodded at long last. "On this point, we agree."

"I want to help him."

"You love him that much?"

She nodded. "Will you wait for me in the car?" With a quick, grim smile Jane excused herself from Zayad and went after Bobby. She found him at the other end of the corral, lightly slapping a dusty pad against the horse's side. She wasted no time, her anger now free to show itself.

"What was that?"

He didn't look at her. "That was pissed off."

"At what? Zayad's done nothing to you."

"It's the attitude, Jane," he said, glancing up, his blue eyes filled with the same ire she always saw when they spoke about the past. "It's the belief that good things come to those who lie and cheat. If someone's going to deceive someone else…" he paused, shook his head.

"What?" asked Jane uneasily. She felt desperate to understand him, help him, heal him. If only he'd let her. If only she could grasp the real Bobby, the one who cared for her, and stamp out the one who hated her family, maybe they'd have a chance.

"Well, they should only expect to get their ears boxed," said Bobby, his fist tight around the pad. "Get what they deserve for hurting someone else."

"When Zayad came to California to see me, he was only trying to find out who I was. He knew that deceiving us about his identity was wrong and immoral, and he asked Mariah and me to forgive him. He's more than paid his debt to Mariah."

Grabbing the rope that had been tossed over the fence, Bobby said sullenly, "The particulars are none of my business."

"Maybe not, but when you make judgments—"

"They're fair judgments, Jane," said Bobby, turning on her, his gaze fierce. "A lie is a lie."

"The world's not that black and white," said Jane in apple-crisp tones.

"It is to me."

She stared at him, her heart pounding furiously in her chest. His conviction for the truth impressed her, but the solid sourness that resided in his eyes made her wince in frustration. "We're obviously at an impasse," she said finally, feeling a wave a gloom move through her gut. Did they even stand a chance of making it? "I'm going to go now."

When she turned on her heel and started away from him, he reached out, grabbed her hand and pulled her back to him. For several moments, he held her close, his breathing slow and steady. Jane closed her eyes and allowed herself to melt into him.

"Darlin'?"

The husky endearment caused the cold navy blue of Jane's heart to warm into a soft pink. "Yes?"

"I'm sorry."

"I know."

"Come back. After you see your friend." He eased back, bent his head and nuzzled her mouth. "I'm an angry bastard, but I need you, Jane. I need you so damn much."

The torture in his voice, the desperation in his tone, and the love she had for him in her heart made her weak. She let him hold her, let his mouth cover hers, let her weariness of spirit turn into a tumbling sense of desire. "I'll be back."

Twisted and confused, Jane pushed away from him. The walk from the corral to the driveway to the man waiting for her in his shiny, black Mercedes was one of the longest and, strangely, the loneliest, of her life.

* * *

"May I say it again?"

Jane laughed at her glowing best friend as they walked down Grand Avenue after their late lunch. The day was slowly turning into evening, but the warm sun filtered through the trees lining the sidewalk with fierce determination. "Okay. Say it again if you feel you must."

With a dramatic sigh, Mariah put a hand to her growing belly and said wistfully, "I miss your tapioca pudding something awful."

Again, Jane laughed, and the sound moved through her like music. Ever since she'd found out that the man living next door to her and Mariah was not only the sultan of a foreign land, but her brother, ever since she'd left her home in California, Jane had been walking on a tenuous cloud. She'd missed the girlfriend banter with her childhood friend. It felt comfortable and familiar and it made her feel as though she could open up in ways she never could in Emand—or at Sakir's home.

"So, no pudding in Emand?" Jane asked.

"Of course," Mariah said as she proceeded to count off on her fingers. "Mango pudding, coconut pudding, the chef even managed a pretty fabulous chocolate pudding. But when he attempted tapioca…" She said no more, only rolled her lips under her teeth and shook her head.

"Well, we'll have to remedy that right now," Jane told her, giving her a wry wink. "But first, butter pecan."

"Oh, I thank you and my baby thanks you," Mariah said with a greedy little giggle as she tucked her arm in Jane's. There was a moment of silence as they headed toward the ice cream shop, then Mariah inhaled and said slowly, "Just so I know, when I do get my pudding, where do I need to pick it up?"

Shaking her head, Jane chuckled. "That was a smooth segue."

"Thank you," said Mariah proudly, flipping her blond hair. "I'm learning quite a bit from Redet, and from that old windbag of a P.R. man at the palace."

"Not to mention the kids you represent in court, right?"

"Kids are the very best at changing the subject—but I have to say that you come in a close second."

Jane gave her friend a wide grin. "All right. I'm staying with Bobby Callahan."

"Yes, I've heard the reports. You sure you know what you're doing?"

"Nope." The unease that had been running through Jane's blood on a daily basis didn't feel nearly as frightening to admit when she was with Mariah. "But I'm in love."

"Yeah, that'll pretty much wipe out all good sense." Mariah wiggled her eyebrows. "And I only know this from personal experience."

"The thing is, he's a good man, Mariah. Loving and kind and sexy and, well…he makes me feel needed and desired. I've never felt like this about anyone in my life. I want to be his other half, share his life here…if he wants me."

"Really? You think you might want to stay in Texas? No Emand with your best friend?"

"Tara is really starting to love it here, and…well," A

warm flush surged into Jane's cheeks and belly. "Emand makes a great honeymoon destination."

Mariah came to an abrupt halt in front of the ice-cream store. Totally unaware of the throngs of people herding in and out of the glass doors with their double scoops and banana splits, she asked, in all seriousness this time, "Do you think he's going to ask you to marry him?"

Jane shook her head. "I honestly don't know. It's what I fantasize about, if that means anything. Bobby cares about me, I know that much. But he has a lot to work through, people to forgive—his father's choices to come to terms with. But the way Sakir and Zayad talk, it'll be a miracle if Bobby and I end up together."

In all good friendships, there comes a point in time when one party needs to hear a word or two of encouragement, whether the other person believes what she's saying or not. This was one of those times, and as always, Mariah curled around her friend in an emotionally indulgent way.

"I don't care what anyone says, Jane—or what they believe to be true. I want you to be happy. If you love this man, then you have to fight for that love, right?"

Hope swelled within Jane and she nodded. "Right."

"Now," Mariah began with a tough smile. "With that said, if Bobby Callahan ever hurts you, Sakir and Zayad will have to climb over me to get to him."

Jane couldn't help herself. She burst out laughing.

"Let's get that ice cream," said Mariah, making for the doors. "If this child doesn't get a nutritious meal soon, he or she is going to kick me into oblivion."

Thirteen

The days leading up to little Daya's Welcome to the World party rolled over on each other like a carpet. By Friday, Jane thought her head might explode with all the information, recipes, times and worries she had crammed into her brain. Her body felt slightly drained from so much prepping, cooking and discussions/arguments with the decorator. But it looked as though the party would go off without a hitch and, though tired, Jane felt very pleased with herself.

Her relationship with Sakir, however, was not doing nearly as well. Jane had wondered if she and her brother would have some time to talk, maybe settle a few matters, since she worked under his roof nearly every day. But Sakir stayed in his office most of the time, and when he did emerge, all he offered her was a quick hello as they passed each other in the house. Even as she was immersed in party planning, she missed their talks, his funny, starchy ways and his brotherly presence.

As she drove away from his home the night before the party, she wondered if they'd ever be friends again, if he'd ever welcome her into his home as his family.

The weathered KC Ranch sign gave her a dusty, encouraging smile as she passed through the gates. If she were to be honest with herself, she'd admit that Sakir's house would only be a place to visit now anyway. How she viewed "home" had changed the moment she'd moved into Bobby's house. Against her better judgment, she'd been referring to the ranch as her home for some time now, and actually felt a thrill when she pulled up and saw the lights flicker in the open windows.

She didn't even bother heading over to the cabin. Three days ago, when Tara and Abel had returned from their night under the stars with looks of total adoration on their happy faces, they'd all made a silent agreement. Tara and Abel would have the cabin and Jane and Bobby would have the house. Sometimes they took meals together, sometimes not. It was smooth and easy and Jane had never seen her mother so happy.

Jane pulled back the screen door and sighed as she entered the house. "Do I smell pizza?"

"You do."

The sight before her was like something out of a dream. Looking thoroughly pleased with himself, Bobby stood beside the couch, big and sexy and rough in his faded jeans and pale-green T-shirt, a delicious smile on his lips. And in front of him, on the coffee table, was a hot mushroom and pepperoni pizza, a bottle of wine and a few videos stacked up on top of each other.

"Oh, I love you!" she said in a rush, then glanced up sheepishly.

Bobby raised an eyebrow and grinned.

"You know what I mean," Jane said, forcing a casual tone to her voice.

"No. What do you mean?"

Acting coy, she strolled over the kitchen table and dropped her things on the rough wood surface. "A starving woman will say anything. She's got a mental block that only nourishment will banish."

"Only nourishment?"

She grinned as she watched him move toward her, take her hand in his. "I didn't say what I was hungry for."

"Yes, you did, darlin'. It's in your eyes." He guided her over to the couch and motioned for her to have a seat. "Haven't eaten a thing all day, have you?"

"I think I had some peanuts around ten," said Jane, dropping onto the soft cushion.

"Pathetic."

"They were organic."

He chuckled, opened the pizza box, took out a slice and slipped it onto a plate. "Here." He handed her the plate, then filled a glass with wine.

As she ate her slice with gusto, she said, "You better be careful, Callahan."

"Why's that?"

"I could get used to this."

With an easy grin, he handed her the glass of wine. "Drink up."

The slow, delicate currant flavor of the merlot went to work in a hurry. Feeling relaxed and happy, Jane fell back against the couch cushions and eyed her hunky cowboy. "I want to ask you something, and I want you to promise to think about it before you fly off the handle."

He snorted. "I don't fly off the handle."

"On this subject you do."

"You want me to teach one of your brothers to ride?" he asked, his eyes filled with grim amusement.

"Something easier than that." She grinned, her eyebrows rising hopefully. "Come to the party tomorrow night."

"No," said Bobby succinctly. He smiled brightly. "See, no flying off the handle."

"There was also none of the suggested thinking, either."

"C'mon, Jane," said Bobby, tossing a second slice of pizza onto his plate. "Why would you want another batch of stress added to your night?"

"I don't. I want you." The limb she was going out on felt shaky, but she pressed on. "I want you there, supporting me."

He sighed.

"All-you-can-eat desserts," she tempted, grinning.

"Even if I did agree, I wouldn't be welcome there."

"You're my guest," said Jane, sliding her plate back on the coffee table and inching closer to him. "All that needs to be said, okay?"

His gaze bored into her, a struggle going on behind his eyes. One she couldn't name. But when she smiled at him, he returned it and shook his head. "All right. One condition."

She gave him a quick kiss, then eased back. "Anything."

He took the glass of wine from her and placed it on the table, then took her in his arms. "The dessert sampling starts tonight."

He had her shirt unbuttoned, bra around her waist and his tongue circling her nipple before she could say another word.

The pearly-gray light outside his bedroom window signaled the dawn of a day he'd both anticipated and dreaded for some time. Until now, Bobby hadn't decided when the day of reckoning—the day he destroyed the woman beside him—would come, but Jane's invitation, her plea for his support last night, had offered him the opportunity on a cold, calculating platter.

Bobby shifted under the sheets, Jane following his movement without waking, her arms tightening around him, making him feel claustrophobic and beloved all at the same time.

He was a monster.

A cold-blooded, unfeeling asshole, and yet he knew he would close all passageways to his heart and follow through with his plan.

He owed it to his father. The final payback. Then maybe he'd be free, be able to breathe again—let go of all the anger that fisted around him.

"It's barely morning," said Jane in a husky whisper against his chest.

"I know." He cuddled her deep into his chest and kissed the top of her dark head. It would be the last time he would feel her beside him. Her warmth, her scent. "Go back to sleep, darlin'."

She was quiet for a moment and he thought she'd fallen asleep, but once again she stirred. "Bobby?"

"Yes?"

"I really do love you, you know."

Bobby died inside.

His gut twisted in pain, a sick, shallow feeling moved through every vein, every bone, every muscle. He wanted to pull away from her, or push her off him before she branded him with her words of love.

But he lay there, listening to her breathing turn slow and shallow as she crept back into sleep.

The mattress felt soft, too soft, ready to swallow him whole, and all he could think about was taking her with him, escaping his burden together.

He stared at the ceiling, at the morning light as it turned from gray to the color of sun-bleached hay. Not only was this the last time he would hold Jane, but also it was the last time she'd ever speak to him with love in her voice. The thought cut him deep.

He never would have believed it.

From one wild night at the Turnbolts' to this, this…something real. He'd just never counted on how much it would hurt to lose her.

Fourteen

"**B**eautiful." "Elegant". "Delicious." "Outstanding."

These were the comments that Jane heard as she walked the ancient Armenian carpets scattered over the hardwood floors of the Al-Nayhals' massive living room. Three crystal chandeliers blazed a lovely light throughout the room, making the bronze statues, Italian and Spanish artwork and the beautiful photograph of Daya and Rita catch the eye.

A young man held out a glass of Cristal to her and smiled. She took it and thanked him. Her staff was exceeding her expectations. With wall-to-wall guests, the servers seemed to be moving at the speed of sound to take care of everyone's drink requests. They were even caring for the children, though the little ones had their own party going on in the corner of the room. Anticipating the needs of the guests' children, Jane had set up a kiddie table, with every yummy treat imaginable, all surrounded by toys, puzzles, crayons and miniature sofas.

Jane glanced over at the extra-long table overflowing with flowers, food and candles set up in the adjoining room and smiled. The room was still packed with people who were going for seconds. The party was a success.

She was a success.

She knew now that her dream of opening a restaurant had been with her all along, had been a part of her, but alas, it had just taken her a while to rediscover that passion. It was hard to see clearly through a fog of sudden insecurity, which was what she had suffered from the moment Zayad had revealed who she was. But now her confidence had returned in a marvelous rush. Now she recognized her future once again. Only one question remained—where would she unlock that dream? Where would she open her restaurant?

With a quick glance in the direction of the entryway, Jane bit her lip. Bobby was supposed to have been here over an hour ago. She'd called the ranch, but there had been no answer. He was not the kind of guy to go back on his word, and she didn't believe he'd come to any harm on his way over here.

Looking gorgeous in a pale-blue silk dress, Rita strolled over to her, baby in her arms and someone Jane could only assume was Rita's sister by her side. "Jane, I'd like you to meet my sister, Ava."

"It's nice to meet you," said Jane, shaking the striking blond woman's hand.

"You, too," Ava said warmly. "I've heard so much about you."

Giving her sister an affectionate smile, Rita told Jane, "Ava brought her husband, Jared, his mother, Muna, and my niece, Lily, but they're out in the gardens right now. You'll meet them later. For now," she said dramatically, "I want Daya to give her auntie a kiss. She's a genius chef."

Daya was fast asleep, and Jane leaned down and brushed a thumb over her soft cheek. "How about I give you one, precious?"

"Seriously, Jane," said Rita warmly, her blue eyes flashing with pleasure. "This is fantastic." And Ava nodded in agreement.

Flushing proudly, Jane said, "I'm glad."

"Sakir thinks so, too." She gave Jane a sheepish smile. "I have a feeling he's making his way over here to tell you so himself."

And when Jane looked past Rita she saw just that. Sakir, shouldered by Zayad, was talking with an older couple a few feet away, though Sakir's gaze kept flickering toward Jane.

"So," Rita said, lowering her voice. "Are you enjoying yourself?"

"Sure." That was almost the same thing as being proud of herself, wasn't it?

Rita glanced at Ava, then back again to Jane. "Well, that's not very convincing."

Jane chuckled. "No, I guess not."

It was true that with every wonderful thing that happened tonight, she missed having Bobby to share it with. Jane tried to think back to this morning and Bobby's mood. She'd been distracted with plans, and had left for Sakir's around nine. But before then, at the breakfast table, Bobby hadn't said much to her. In fact, he'd had a tense expression on his face when she'd kissed him goodbye.

A cold shiver moved up her spine, and she reached in her purse for her cell phone. But Rita's words and the smile that accompanied it stopped her.

"Someone is here to see you, Jane."

Jane glanced toward the doorway. Relief spread over her, along with a wave of possessiveness. He'd come. For her, he'd braved the censure of her brother and come.

Dressed simply for a semi-formal affair in black jeans and a white shirt, he still looked overbearing and sexy, though more than a little tense. But that was to be expected as a guest of Sakir Al-Nayhal.

She quickly smoothed down the skirt of her pale-gold silk dress and gave him her most charming smile. She could feel Sakir's and Zayad's eyes on her, but she didn't care. All she could think about was telling Bobby of her success here tonight, of how rooted and self-confident she felt again—how she finally understood where her career was going.

His mouth set in a tense line, Bobby strode right up to her, didn't acknowledge Rita, Ava or Mariah, who had just joined them.

"You look handsome tonight, Mr. Callahan," she said, reaching for his hand. "Thank you for coming."

But he didn't give her his hand, and there was something strange in his gaze, something blank—almost dead. "I have something to say to you."

His cold tone hit her hard, made her shiver. "Okay."

Around her, the small gang of women seemed to stop breathing, and Jane's heart began to thump loudly in her chest as the taste of fear blocked out her earlier taste of success.

"These past few weeks have been a mistake," said Bobby roughly. "I wanted you and I took you, but that's all there was."

Someone put a supportive arm around her waist, but in her shock, Jane couldn't tell who it was.

"I've come here to tell you that I don't want you anymore, Jane."

Their gazes clashed and held, and the shock evaporated from Jane's mind. Through gritted teeth, she uttered, "Is that so?"

He nodded. "I could never love you."

"You're probably right," Jane countered, realizing with a flash just what was happening here, what Bobby Callahan was doing.

"I think you should leave, Mr. Callahan," said Rita in a disgusted voice.

He nodded, but not at Rita, at Jane. And for one brief second she swore she detected a flash of misery in his lifeless gaze, but it was gone in an instant.

And so was Bobby Callahan.

Anger unlike anything she had ever known flooded Jane's senses as she watched him walk away. Around her, Rita, Ava and Mariah were trying to comfort her, offering answers and angry excuses for Bobby's insanity and flagrant disregard for her feelings. But Jane wasn't listening. She shoved her gaze to where Sakir and Zayad stood just feet away. They weren't talking to the older couple anymore. Zayad looked murderous and ready to spring. Sakir was staring at Jane, a brother's grief in his eyes.

She pushed away from her family and headed after Bobby. If he really didn't want her, fine. But that's not what was going on here, and she was going to make him face that truth before he walked away from what they had so easily.

"Jane," she heard Sakir call after her as she rushed to the front door and yanked it open.

"I don't have time right now, Sakir."

"I am sorry."

She whirled around, her anger at Bobby—at this whole stupid, wasteful situation—coming to a head. "For what exactly? Not being able to rub Bobby's rejection in my face, or for pushing me out of your life when I was just getting used to having a brother?"

She watched the effect of her words as they burned into his face, made his lips thin and his jaw tighten. "I could not see you get hurt."

"Well, you see it now, don't you?" she countered, feeling the cool night air wash over her heated skin and temper. "What's the difference?"

When he didn't answer, she turned around and fled down the front steps toward her rental car.

"Jane. Wait."

With a sigh, she managed one last glance over her shoulder. "What?"

His green eyes heavy with concern, Sakir asked, "Where are you going?"

"To help one stupid man get over the past once and for all. Maybe while I'm gone the other man will have the balls to get over it, too."

She left Sakir with his mouth hanging open.

A first.

There wasn't enough alcohol in the whole state of Texas to block out the words he'd just uttered to Jane. Or the look on her face when he'd said them. So Bobby remained sober, his gut, soul and what remained of his heart aching.

In the shelter of the barn, he sat on a pile of fragrant hay, in the back of an empty stall and wondered when the relief of a vow completed would overtake him.

Would it be tomorrow? Next week? Next year?

Ever?

Or would this new pain, this loss of a woman who had come to mean everything to him take the place of his grief over losing his father and sister?

"So, did it work?"

Only mildly startled, he glanced up, saw an angel dressed in pale gold, her dark hair swirling around her shoulders, her eyes filled with a passion he understood only too well. "Did what work?"

"Your plan."

"I don't know what you're talking about."

"Get off it, Bobby. The plan to win back your self-respect and gain a little revenge in the process?"

"Why are you here?"

She ignored his question, moved farther into the stall. "Please tell me that you're happy now."

He cursed, forgot his stoic, unaffected mood and just let loose. "The plan was never to be happy, darlin'. I'll never be happy. But yes, I've finally avenged my family's honor by destroying your brother's family."

Jane cocked her head to the side. "My family's not destroyed." She shook her head. "Yes, you hurt me. Deeply and intolerably. But my family's fine."

"Even you and Sakir?" he asked darkly.

She flinched, but steadied herself and lifted her chin. "Maybe not today or tomorrow, but we'll get over it, and I'll forgive him for being a jerk."

She'd forgive him, but no doubt she'd never forgive Bobby. So, Al-Nayhal would win once again. Land, livelihood and the girl of Bobby's dreams. "So, through all the lies comes a happy ending for the Al-Nayhals," he spat out, wishing now he had gotten disgustingly drunk. "Figures."

"Don't speak to me about lies, Callahan," she countered angrily. "What did you say the other day? 'If someone's going to deceive someone else they should expect to get their ears boxed? Get what they deserve for hurting someone else?'"

"Damn right." He scrambled to his feet and stalked over to her, his heart slamming against his ribs. "Hit me."

"Don't tempt me."

He stood close to her, the heat of their bodies intense. He wanted to pull her into his arms, make love to her mouth, make them both forget what had happened tonight, but he knew that was impossible.

She stared at him with those large green eyes. "I want you to face the truth, your past and all those demons that drive you, and move on."

"I did that tonight."

"No, you acted like a child tonight. It takes a man to stand up for what he really wants and to say to hell with anyone who asks you to deny it."

Bobby froze where he stood. No one had ever said anything like that to him—called him a child. The words made his blood boil, made his mind go numb. He was no child. He was a man who had to make good on a promise, and that was that.

"Is there anything more you want to say, Jane?" he asked, icicles clinging to his tone.

He saw her chin tremble, her eyes fill with tears, but she shook her head, looked up until the tears were gone. When she found his gaze again, she said softly, simply, "I love you, Bobby. I may be a fool for saying it, for coming here, trying again…"

The words, and the tender, devoted tone in her voice, pierced his hard, cold shell—but what followed had every muscle in his body stiff with ire.

"I want you as my family."

As memories of his father, his sister and the battles he'd had with Sakir Al-Nayhal over the years slammed into his mind, Bobby felt his face contort into a mask of rage.

A member of the Al-Nayhal family!

Teeth gritted, he practically hissed, "I'd rather die first."

He watched as the blood drained from Jane's face,

the breath squeezed from her body. Hands shaking, eyes filling with tears once again, she said clearly, "If I leave here, I'm not coming back."

The full impact of her words was lost on Bobby. All he felt was hatred for her brother in that moment, not the love that surely dwelled in his heart. "Goodbye, Jane."

Tears slipping down her face, Jane nodded. "I'll get my things and be out of here in no time."

She turned around and walked away.

And he was alone.

Again.

The airplane engines rumbled, readying themselves for takeoff. With a book lying open and unread on her lap, Jane stared out the window, and wished she were already in Emand. The long flight would be difficult with nothing to do but think about what had happened last night, what had been said at the party and in Bobby's barn. There was also no one to talk to on the flight, to keep her mind occupied with trivial matters. Due to a few business engagements, Mariah and Zayad hadn't been ready to leave, but had offered Jane the private plane, understanding her haste to get away. Jane's mother had suggested that she go with her, but Jane could plainly see that Tara was in love with Abel, and wanted to remain with him. Jane had told her mother that she would call her when she got to Emand, and they could decide what to do from there. Sakir, on the other hand, had tried to reason with Jane, urging her to stay at his home until she figured out what she wanted.

But Jane was determined.

Right now, she needed as much distance as possible between herself and Bobby Callahan. Odds were she wouldn't get over him in a lifetime, but the thousands of miles, oceans and deserts might help a little.

She closed her eyes, knowing that the events of last night would play in her mind and ears. Sinking into the grief, Jane let the shots and jabs he'd uttered, his eyes dark with a lifetime of indignation, poke at her. He'd rather die than be her family. He wanted nothing to do with her.

She believed it all.

Except for one thing.

She knew he loved her, and that truth hurt worst of all. Bobby Callahan could love her and yet dump her because of her family.

She supposed she hadn't really known him at all.

Around her, the airplane's engines whirled, the tires rotated and they were off down the runway and away from Paradise, Texas.

Fifteen

"**Y**ou got a death wish, Al-Nayhal?"

It had been one week since Jane had left, since Bobby had exacted his revenge, and had put an end to his duty to his father. He'd expected to feel a helluva lot lighter, at peace, maybe. But he only felt angrier, raw, as though he'd like very much to slam his fist through a wall—or through the man standing before him wearing a white kaftan and an arrogant expression.

Looking perfectly out of place in KC Ranch's dusty barn, Sakir lifted his chin. "Do not toss about threats you cannot possibly follow through on."

Bobby stabbed his pitchfork into a mound of hay. "Oh, I can follow through."

Sakir glanced at the makeshift weapon as though it were a thin twig. "As much as I would love to demon-

strate all my years of training with both sword and staff,
I have more important matters to discuss."

The sight of the man made Bobby's blood boil, made
him think about Jane. "Make it quick. You're trespass-
ing, and I have work to do."

"I have brought you this."

Bobby eyed the sheets of white paper Al-Nayhal
thrust toward him. "What is it? Something to force me
off this land now?"

It appeared as though Sakir were trying to hold on to
his patience. "Something that will help you to understand why this land was lost in the first place."

A heaviness settled in Bobby's gut. "What the hell
are you talking about? I know why we lost this land."

"You know only part of the reason." When Bobby
said nothing, Sakir's eyebrow lifted. "Are you going to
take this or not?"

With an indignant growl, Bobby fairly ripped the papers from Sakir's hand. His eyes scanned the docu-
ments. The first was a statement from the drilling
company who had botched the job on his land, claim-
ing they had no affiliation whatsoever with Al-Nayhal
Corporation, squashing Bobby's almost decade-long
conspiracy theory. The other papers consisted of five no-
tices from environmental agencies warning Bobby's father about the instability of the land, warning him that
if actions weren't taken to bring the land up to code, he
would never be allowed to run cattle or horses, or to drill
on his land.

A slow sick feeling came over Bobby as he stared at
the date of the first and second notice. Six years before

his father had lost the property. And he'd still allowed drilling, knowing what could happen, knowing that the drilling could ruin not only the land, but also his family. And afterward, the man had forced Bobby to come home from the road—a life he'd loved with all his heart—to fix a problem that could have been fixed long before.

And through it all, his father had made him believe that Sakir Al-Nayhal was to blame. Worse still, his father had made Bobby promise to carry a burden of revenge for years—while life went on around him, while a woman had found him and helped him to breathe, love life and care about someone again.

Bobby's hand fisted around the papers. If this was true, Bobby's father could have saved the property. If this was true, Kimmy and Bobby would have had their home without having to beg for a tiny portion of it back.

"Mr. Callahan, I—" Sakir began, but was cut off.

"This is a fake," said Bobby, unwilling to believe that his father would have done something like this. The man had been a great father, a good rancher, a respected member of the community. "You have the money to do it, and you'll stop at nothing to defame my father—"

Sakir actually appeared empathetic. "You can check for yourself. Local county offices and state offices have all these records on file."

Bobby started to shake, with fury for his father, for Sakir, for himself and for Jane. But the anger in his heart came out as anguish in his tone. "If this is really true, why would you keep this a secret? Why wouldn't you tell me? I spent years blaming you…."

With a heavy sigh, Sakir said, "I loved my father. I did not want to know of his mistakes or misdeeds. You and your sister thought much of your father." He shrugged, though his chin never dropped. "I thought it best you both hate me and not him."

Bobby couldn't believe what he was hearing. There was no way that Sakir Al-Nayhal was a good guy. No way! Bobby had spent too many years despising him. "And why are you telling me this now? After all these years?"

"I never thought you would try and avenge your father with something I could not handle." Sakir's eyes darkened. "My sister's heart is something I cannot control."

Jane. His beloved Jane. Caught up in a scheme based on lies told by an old man because he didn't want to deal with his mistakes. Bobby fell against the stall door and stared at the rafters.

"I love my sister, Mr. Callahan. And she loves you. I will not attempt to make choices for her again."

Shaking his head, Bobby uttered, "She said she'll never step foot on my land again."

"No, but perhaps if you went to her first."

Bobby came awake in an instant. "Emand?"

Sakir nodded. "It is her land now. Perhaps you will both find peace there."

The palace gardens were scented with citrus and roses, a heavenly combination that sought to soothe Jane's restless mind. But neither the roses nor the spectacular pink sunset before her could manage to curb her sadness. It had been this way for almost two weeks, she mused dejectedly as she sat on an iron bench and sipped her tea. She hated herself for feeling so downcast, missing Bobby the way she did, as though he were an appendage that still felt very much attached.

If she were wise, she'd force him to the back of her mind and concentrate on her future. Over the past week, she'd managed to make a list of restaurants, all bearing her name, some menu ideas, even thoughts on decor. But what she couldn't get down on paper was where this restaurant might be.

"Hi, sweetie."

Jane glanced up and saw her mother on the arm of Abel Garret walking toward her. Tara and Abel had arrived two days ago. Jane hadn't been surprised to see Abel with her mother when Jane had met them at the airplane. The two were most definitely inseparable, and their obvious devotion to one another made Jane's heart seize up every time she saw them.

"We have a surprise for you, Janie," said Abel, tossing her a crooked grin.

Jane returned the smile, half-hearted though it was. "Thank you, guys, but I'm not really up for surprises today." Or any day, for that matter.

"You'll love this one," Tara said with deep conviction, then glanced over her shoulder.

The low, masculine voice echoed throughout the garden, causing all the night insects to still. "You said you wouldn't come to me, so I came to you."

Jane's heart dropped into her shoes, and she whirled around. The man coming toward her was dressed in jeans and a pale-blue shirt, his chest as wide as the pathway on which he walked. His eyes glowed with regret and happiness and love, and his look nearly caused Jane to break down into tears.

Without a word, Abel and Tara slipped away, and Bobby Callahan stood before her. He took a deep breath, his gaze moving possessively over every inch of her until at last, he stared into her eyes. "You look beautiful."

"Bobby…"

"God, I've missed you. I've never ached like this before, in my body and my soul."

She knew exactly what he meant. Nights of loneliness and endless days with nothing to look forward to, a deep ache that nothing would ease. But Bobby had hurt her beyond measure, and no matter how much she still loved him, he wouldn't gain her forgiveness easily.

As if he saw the reticent glow in her eyes, he nodded. "I don't deserve this, just standing before you."

Jane's gaze flickered, her legs felt suddenly water-filled.

"I don't deserve it, but I'm taking it because I love you, Jane. I love you with every part of me, and I had to tell you so. I had to come here and apologize for what I did to you and your family." He reached out, tentatively brushed her hand. His eyes were a deep shade of blue. "Oh, Jane, darlin'. You belong back in Paradise. We belong together. You belong with me."

"I don't know if I do," she uttered, pain slashing her heart, tears pricking her eyes. "I'm scared, Bobby. I gave you everything, my love and trust…my heart and soul, and you tore them up and threw them back in my face. How am I supposed to believe in you again?"

Pain flickered in his eyes. "I'm not asking you to believe in me, Jane. But maybe you could believe in us."

Tears fell down her cheeks.

"Hear me out, darlin', please," he beseeched her, taking her hands in his, his eyes imploring to listen—really hear him. "Guilt and shame are funny things. They make you desperate. They make you do things that you know are wrong. They make you hurt people you love. In my case, they made me turn a blind eye to the weakness of a father I loved dearly, a man I wanted to believe was beyond reproach. A man I was sure had put the needs of his family ahead of his own."

The undisguised misery in his eyes made her heart ache, her throat tighten.

"I made a vow to my father on his deathbed," Bobby continued to say, "to avenge his honor, to hurt the Al-Nayhals as we'd been hurt." He shook his head. "I didn't know the truth of it. I didn't know that it was really my father, through all his mistakes, his blind eye, who had lost our land. I didn't want to believe that. Neither did he, obviously. He was a good man, Jane. He was Kimmy's savior, her touchstone. It broke her heart when he died. Mine, too. So, I blamed Sakir for every one of my losses." With a curse, Bobby pulled her into his arms. "I'm so sorry. I was such a fool. I hurt you, pushed you away after the love and the life you gave me, gave back to me, really. God, you'll never know how sorry I am."

"Yes, I do." Jane couldn't stop the tears, the sobs. She cried against his chest.

He held her for a moment, rocked her, crushed her in his embrace. "Will you forgive me, Jane? Can you forgive me? All I ask for is another chance." He placed a finger under her chin and lifted her bleary-eyed gaze to his. "I want to be your family. I want the babies we're going to have. I want you." With the pad of his thumb, he wiped a fat tear from her cheek. "I love you."

Even through tears, through the pain of what had been said in the past, Jane felt alive and tall and purposeful for the first time in almost two weeks. She understood his past, and now, so did he. When she spoke, her voice rang true and joyful. "I love you. More than ever, and I know what's in your heart. I see it."

A smile broke out on his face, so bright with relief and adoration it squeezed at Jane's heart. "Marry me, darlin'," said Bobby, lowering his head, giving her a tender kiss. "Marry me and teach me everyday how to be a better man."

His words gripped her tightly, curled around her, made her feel safe and filled with love. Finding his way through a wounded past, Bobby's heart had finally opened. He was ready to embrace a future, and Jane knew where she belonged—in his arms, her mouth to his, their breath as one.

"Yes," she whispered between kisses as the pink sun slowly set before them. "We will teach each other, my love."

Epilogue

Six months later

"Do you take this man to be your husband?"

Jane held her breath, her heart seizing with emotion. She'd always wanted this day to come, always hoped that there was a future to look forward to.

Standing proudly at the makeshift altar, Tara smiled at Abel and said, "I do."

"Then I pronounce you husband and wife," the preacher said with a wide smile. "You may kiss your bride, Abel."

In the field beside the lake where Bobby and Jane had swum, and where Abel and Tara had looked at the stars in their own beautiful way, two people committed their lives to one another.

Bobby took Jane's hand in his and squeezed it, his own wedding band rubbing softly against her fingers. "Want to do that all over again?"

Remembering their emotional wedding ceremony in Emand a month earlier, Jane grinned at her husband as he lifted her onto his gray stallion. "In a heartbeat. But maybe we should wait until our anniversary."

Climbing up behind her, Bobby kissed her ear and whispered, "It is our anniversary. One month today."

She snuggled against him as they rode back to the ranch house, back home, all of their family and friends behind them. "Who'd have believed that a six-foot-three, barrel-chested cowboy would be such a romantic?" she called over her shoulder.

"Anyone who looks at the woman he's married to," Bobby shouted over the thunder of horse's hooves.

"I love you, Bobby Callahan."

"I love you, and tonight we're going to say those vows all over again." As Rip galloped beneath them, Bobby held her tightly to his chest, brushed a kiss over her ear and uttered, "When I'm inside you."

She laughed, true happiness enveloping her as the fresh Texas air pelted her face. "I'm not sure I can wait until tonight for that."

"'Fraid you'll have to, darlin'," Bobby said as they pulled up to the ranch house, and the brand-new structure beside it. "Got a wedding feast to go to. And it's at my favorite restaurant in town."

Her heart full, Jane stared up at the sign above the

restaurant, her restaurant. "It's not set to open for three weeks. How is it your favorite already?"

He winked at her. "I've sampled the goods."

Around them, the whole gang, her whole new family rode up to The Darlin', ready and hungry for a full Texas feast. It was beyond her wildest imaginings, but Jane had everything she'd ever wanted—Bobby, a restaurant of her own and a true purpose, as KC Ranch was expanding, taking on more students, staff and wonderful programs. And Jane would nourish them all not only with her food, but her heart.

"Do I smell cornbread?" Ava's husband Jared asked as he jumped down from his horse.

"I love cornbread," said their daughter Lily, still sitting in front of her grandmother Muna, who cooed at the girl and said, "You just love food, Little Star."

"Like the rest of her family," Rita commented, stepping out of her car and handing Daya to Sakir, who promptly kissed the little girl's forehead.

"You did make coleslaw, my sister?" Zayad asked, helping Mariah from the same car as she was too pregnant to ride a horse now. "I do so enjoy that salad."

"Hope you made that brisket of yours," called Abel as he walked up the restaurant steps hand in hand with his new bride.

After assuring them all that their Texas favorites had indeed been prepared, Jane escaped into The Darlin' and into her beloved kitchen. And as she removed macaroni and cheese, beef brisket, potatoes and a chocolate sheet cake from their respective ovens, she smiled. Crowding noisily into her restaurant was her family. Happy, healthy and so much wiser.

Her heart swelled. She did indeed have it all.

* * * * *

If you enjoyed what you just read,
then we've got an offer you can't resist!

Take 2 bestselling
love stories FREE!
Plus get a FREE surprise gift!

Clip this page and mail it to Silhouette Reader Service™

IN U.S.A.	**IN CANADA**
3010 Walden Ave.	P.O. Box 609
P.O. Box 1867	Fort Erie, Ontario
Buffalo, N.Y. 14240-1867	L2A 5X3

YES! Please send me 2 free Silhouette Desire® novels and my free surprise gift. After receiving them, if I don't wish to receive anymore, I can return the shipping statement marked cancel. If I don't cancel, I will receive 6 brand-new novels every month, before they're available in stores! In the U.S.A., bill me at the bargain price of $3.80 plus 25¢ shipping and handling per book and applicable sales tax, if any*. In Canada, bill me at the bargain price of $4.47 plus 25¢ shipping and handling per book and applicable taxes**. That's the complete price and a savings of at least 10% off the cover prices—what a great deal! I understand that accepting the 2 free books and gift places me under no obligation ever to buy any books. I can always return a shipment and cancel at any time. Even if I never buy another book from Silhouette, the 2 free books and gift are mine to keep forever.

225 SDN DZ9F
326 SDN DZ9G

Name	(PLEASE PRINT)	
Address	Apt.#	
City	State/Prov.	Zip/Postal Code

Not valid to current Silhouette Desire® subscribers.

Want to try two free books from another series?
Call 1-800-873-8635 or visit www.morefreebooks.com.

* Terms and prices subject to change without notice. Sales tax applicable in N.Y.
** Canadian residents will be charged applicable provincial taxes and GST.
   All orders subject to approval. Offer limited to one per household.
   ® are registered trademarks owned and used by the trademark owner and or its licensee.

DES04R   ©2004 Harlequin Enterprises Limited

**brings you an unforgettable
new miniseries from author**

Linda Conrad

The Gypsy Inheritance

A secret legacy unleashes passion…and promises.

Scandal and seduction go hand in hand as three
powerful men receive unexpected gifts….

SEDUCTION
BY THE BOOK

August 2005
Silhouette Desire #1673

REFLECTED PLEASURES

September 2005
Silhouette Desire #1679

A SCANDALOUS
MELODY

October 2005
Silhouette Desire #1684

Available at your favorite retail outlet.

SDTGI0805

THE SECRET DIARY

A new drama unfolds for six of the state's wealthiest bachelors.

This newest installment continues with

STRICTLY CONFIDENTIAL ATTRACTION

by Brenda Jackson

(Silhouette Desire #1677)

How can you keep a secret when you're living in close quarters? Alison Lind vowed never to reveal her feelings for her boss, Mark Hartman. But that was before she started filling in as nanny to his niece and sleeping just down the hall....

*Available September 2005
at your favorite retail outlet.*

COMING NEXT MONTH

#1675 CONDITION OF MARRIAGE—Emilie Rose
Dynasties: The Ashtons
Abandoned by her lover, pregnant Mercedes Ashton turned to her good friend Jared Maxwell for help. Jared offered her a marriage of convenience…that soon flared into unexpected passion. But when the father of Mercedes's unborn child returned, would her bond with Jared be enough to keep their marriage together?

#1676 TANNER TIES—Peggy Moreland
The Tanners of Texas
Lauren Tanner was determined to get her life back on track…without the assistance of her estranged family. When she hired quiet Luke Jordan, she had no idea the scarred handyman was tied to the Tanners and prepared to use any method necessary—even seduction—to bring Lauren back into the fold.

#1677 STRICTLY CONFIDENTIAL ATTRACTION—
Brenda Jackson
Texas Cattleman's Club: The Secret Diary
Although rancher Mark Hartman's relationship with his attractive secretary, Alison Lind, had always been strictly professional, it changed when he was forced to enlist her aid in caring for his infant niece. Now their business arrangement was venturing into personal—and potentially dangerous—territory.…

#1678 APACHE NIGHTS—Sheri WhiteFeather
Their attraction was undeniable. But neither police detective Joyce Riggs nor skirting-the-edge-of-the-law Apache Kyle Prescott believed there could be anything more than passion between them. They decided the answer to their dilemma was a no-strings affair. That was their first mistake.

#1679 REFLECTED PLEASURES—Linda Conrad
The Gypsy Inheritance
Fashion model Merrill Davis-Ross wanted out of the spotlight and had reinvented herself as the new plain-Jane assistant of billionaire Texan Tyson Steele. But her mission to leave her past behind was challenged when Tyson dared to look beyond Merrill's facade to find the real woman underneath.

#1680 THE RICH STRANGER—Bronwyn Jameson
Princes of the Outback
When fate stranded Australian playboy Rafe Carlisle on her cattle station, usually wary Cat McConnell knew she'd never met anyone like this rich stranger. Because his wild and winning ways tempted her to say yes to night after night of passion, to a temporary marriage—and even to having his baby!

SDCNM0805